Riders From Hell

It is the early 1880s. Tom and Marie Flint have moved to New Mexico and established a small but thriving cattle business. All seems to be going well until the bank in El Jango is robbed and two innocent men are killed by the bank robbers. As they make their escape, the robbers hold up the Santa Fe stage and the Flints' elder son is murdered.

The bank robbers leave a revenge note, calling themselves The Regulators. It seems that the leaders of the bank robbers are intent on destroying the Flint family out of revenge for things that happened in Arkansas over twenty years before.

Tom Flint and his younger son Jason are drawn into a desperate feud with the so-called Regulators and this becomes a battle to the death. But whose death?

Riders From Hell

Lee Lejeune

A Black Horse Western

ROBERT HALE · LONDON

© Lee Lejeune 2008
First published in Great Britain 2008

ISBN 978-0-7090-8579-9

Robert Hale Limited
Clerkenwell House
Clerkenwell Green
London EC1R 0HT

www.halebooks.com

Typeset by
Derek Doyle & Associates, Shaw Heath
Printed and bound in Great Britain by
Antony Rowe Limited, Wiltshire

CHAPTER ONE

The day they busted the bank in El Jango Tom Flint was due to meet with John Chisum in Frenchy's diner. The bank-tellers were drinking cooling beer behind the counter in the bank. It was hot enough in the sun to roast a man, and the dogs lay snoozing under benches in the shade.

Sheriff Cassidy was locked in his own jail.

His story was he had intended to make up his accounts. He had his account book open on his desk with his head down sideways on the page. His mouth was open and he had dribbled over the latest entry, blurring the figures so you could scarcely read them. When he snorted and woke himself, he looked up to see a man standing right in front of him.

The man had slipped in so quietly he might have been a phantom. He wore black leathers and he had a red bandanna covering his nose and jaw; so all you saw was his eyes, which were burning like hot coals. And he was pointing a six-gun at Cassidy.

'Easy there, Sheriff,' the man growled. 'You move

real slow and do what I say or I might have to blow your head off your shoulders. Are you with me, Sheriff?'

It wasn't exactly a question, more of a command. According to Cassidy he didn't reply in words. He just nodded and kept himself very still to indicate he understood.

'There's a good boy,' the man with the red bandanna purred. Cassidy could see the suck and blow of the bandanna when he breathed in and out, but his eyes continued to burn with hostile intent.

'He would have shot me easy as killing a pesky fly,' Cassidy said later.

The sheriff was young and boyish, maybe not more than twenty-five, and they had pinned the badge on him because he came with good references. They said he'd foiled a robbery somewhere close to the Mexican border. Anyway, there wasn't much call for a sheriff in El Jango – not until now. The older sheriff, a man called Reno Bear, had died while out hunting buffalo, when he pitched off his horse on to his head. Not much of a sheriff, and not much of a rider, either!

According to Cassidy the man with the red bandanna pulled over his lower face said: 'Slide over the keys and get yourself in that empty cell and everything's going to be all hunky-dory. You savvy?'

Cassidy did savvy. He had a Smith & Wesson .38 in the drawer but he knew if he made a play for it he was dead meat. So he took the keys down from the peg and slid them over the desk real easy in case the man with the gun got the wrong idea.

The man toting the gun was slim and about five ten.

He picked up the keys, tossed them in his hand and made a motion for Cassidy to step into the cell. There were two cells back of the sheriff's office. Sometimes one was occupied by a drunk or a brawler. That day both were unoccupied.

'What do you aim to do?' Cassidy asked as the man turned the key on him.

According to him the man in the red bandanna gave a nasty chuckle that sounded like boulders crashing in an avalanche into a mountain steam. 'Now you don't want to worry your curly head about that, son. Just settle you down for an afternoon nap like every other respectable citizen in El Jango. That way nobody is going to get hurt none.'

That was the story Cassidy told later.

The man with the red bandanna had given Cassidy a reassuring message but things didn't turn out quite that way. In the bank the tellers were still drinking cool beer behind the counter while the manager snoozed in his office under the most recent edition of the *Las Vegas Gazette*. First thing he heard was someone he took to be a customer talking low to the tellers.

Next thing he knew they were swarming all over the place, men with guns, big burly men bawling at the tellers, ordering them to fill their sacks with dollars, gold, whatever there was. When interrogated later he said: 'There must have been at least twenty of them with guns and I feared for my life!' In fact, there were four bank-robbers and one outside tending the horses.

The manager had reason to be scared. Jerry Todd,

one of the tellers drinking cold beer, went mad with terror when the gunmen appeared.

'Stop fooling around!' he shouted. 'You can't come in here waving those guns about. It ain't decent.' He started gesturing with his arms and threatening to call the manager.

'Fooling nothing!' muttered one of the robbers, and shot him dead.

'Without a qualm!' the manager said later. 'They shot Jerry without a word of remorse. Just like he was a mad steer or something. That's the way they shot him, without a qualm!'

Poor Jerry Todd was a family man with two children, but he just slid down behind the counter and lay gasping his life out.

On the other side of the street a war veteran, Jim Stacey, was dozing under a canopy. He was probably dreaming about his exploits in the war but nobody had a chance to find out. He woke up with a start when he heard the shot and saw the robbers spilling out of the bank with their sacks of loot and their guns pointing every which way. Stacey was a man with a high sense of social responsibility, a solid citizen, and that's what killed him. As the robbers ran down the boardwalk, he dragged his Winchester out from under his chair and stepped forward to challenge them. It was Jim Stacey's last battle and almost his last breath. As he raised the Winchester and made to call out his challenge, one of the robbers turned and shot him clean in the chest. Stacey fell back beside his chair, kicking but dead, with no more than a squeak of protest.

The robbery was all over before the dogs could bark. There were few witnesses other than young Baldy Barlow who was, at that time, reckoned to be two cents short of a dollar and who walked with a sideways lurch like he might keel over and fall at every other step. Baldy had seen everything but, unlike Jim Stacey, he had had the good sense to crouch down and pretend he wasn't there. And Baldy was reckoned to be no gunman, anyway.

'What in tarnation's been happening here?' Joe Slocum the mayor demanded, looking wild-eyed in every direction. It was a needless question. The bank manager stood trembling at the door of the bank with a face as yellow as last week's *Gazette*.

'They robbed the bank!' he cried. 'These men just robbed the bank!'

The second teller was cowering beside him. 'They killed Jerry!' he shrieked. 'Just shot him down right in front of me like a dawg! Jerry was a good man! Wouldn't hurt nobody! Didn't even have a gun!'

Joe Slocum was staring down at the body of Jim Stacey, who was still clutching his Winchester. Stacey's mouth was wide open as though in astonishment and he seemed to be staring at some invisible point in the sky.

'They shot that poor man down,' Baldy Barlow said. 'I seen the whole thing.'

At that point nobody took much notice of Baldy. After all, he was just El Jango's town idiot and everyone knew he slobbered and jabbered, mostly nonsense.

The mayor was still looking all round in dismay. By

now quite a crowd of residents had appeared to stare at Stacey's body.

'Where the hell's the sheriff?' roared the mayor.

'Sheriff's in his office,' Baldy said. 'I seen a man go in there no more than a few minutes past.' Though he spoke in a strange lisping tone and usually nobody took notice of him, this time the mayor looked at him in disbelief.

'What d'you mean, the sheriff's in his office, you damned halfwit. There's been a crime committed here and two men have been murdered. This is where the sheriff should be right now. He should be riding out to apprehend those villains!'

Someone had had the sense to look into the sheriff's office where Cassidy was shaking the bars and acting like a demented gorilla in a zoo.

'Baldy's right,' the man shouted. 'Cassidy's locked in his own jail. We're looking for the key.'

They found the sheriff's keys thrown behind the desk in the office.

If the situation hadn't been tragic some unkind people might have laughed. Cassidy did look like some-thing between an ape and a chimpanzee struggling to pull down the bars in his own jail.

And Baldy Barlow wasn't quite as stupid as some thought he was!

Tom Flint was eating beans and a steak on the rare side and drinking cool beer in Frenchy's diner. He was sitting opposite John Chisum who was also tackling a steak but with no beans, and he was drinking rye. Both were ranchers. Chisum had the biggest spread around the Pecos River. He had built himself up from nothing and was right proud of his achievements and his high social position. Flint's ranch was more modest. He had ridden west to New Mexico back in 1862 with Marie and they had started their spread with nothing but a handful of dollars. Flint and Chisum met occasionally to talk over matters of mutual interest like round-up, the rustling of cattle, and the cattle-drive north along the Goodnight–Loving trail.

At that point Chisum was going on about rustlers and the stock he was losing. 'We've lost a damned sight too many head of cattle to those thieving Mexicans,' he shouted between mouthfuls.

Tom Flint chewed on. 'We lost a few,' he agreed. Because he had experienced hardship himself, he knew what it was like to feel the temptations that come with an empty belly.

'We catch them, we hang them,' Chisum said. 'That's a natural law of nature.'

Tom Flint grinned. 'My son Jason would agree with you,' he conceded. Jason was his younger boy, better at doing things than reasoning about them.

'Damn right, he would!' Chisum exploded. 'Jason's a good boy. He'll be a dang good rancher when you hang up your spurs.'

Flint stuck his head on one side. 'In principle I agree about hanging rustlers. But sometimes practice can be different from principle, you know, John.'

Chisum looked like he would spit out his steak. 'How the hell can that be? Where's the logic in that? If a thing's right, it's damned right and there's no two ways about it.'

Flint chewed on in silence for a moment. 'Like when a starving Mexican steals a cow. Man called Logan caught a Mexican trailing off one of his mangy cows. Strung him up immediately. That might be a little extreme, don't you think?'

Chisum glared at him and then thumped down hard with his fist on the table, causing Frenchy to stare at him in alarm from behind the counter. 'Logan was right,' Chisum thundered. 'Logan's a man of principle and he has a wife and family to consider. He's a good man, Logan is!'

He fell on his steak again with the relish of self-righteousness.

'By the way,' he said, 'Where's your good woman? Thought I saw her ride into town with you on the buckboard?'

'You did,' Flint said with quiet humour. 'Marie's choosing herself a new hat over at Madame Renoir's. Wants to be presentable when the stage comes in.'

'What's with the stage?' Chisum asked.

Flint gave him a cautious glance. He had never completely trusted or liked Chisum and suspected the man would swallow him with his steak if he thought he could digest him. 'Tom junior's with the stage,' he said. 'Riding in from Santa Fe. He's studying the law up there.'

Chisum chuckled. 'So Marie wants to welcome him home like the prodigal son?'

'Something like that,' Tom Flint said, though he

12

wasn't too happy about the biblical reference. His elder son, Tom junior, wasn't a ranching man. He liked to have his nose in a book. Flint was proud of that. Tom junior might end up as a senator or something one day. Young Jason, his younger son, was different altogether. He was a tearaway just as Flint had been in his youth, though he did like working on the ranch and would probably inherit it one day as Chisum had suggested.

Before the two men could continue their conversation they heard the shots, one muffled and the other real loud.

'Sounds like Cassidy's getting in some target practice,' Chisum said contemptuously.

Flint wasn't too sure about that, though it was well known that Cassidy popped bottles off a wall behind his office when he had nothing better to do. He called it *practising for the big one.*

Flint placed his knife and fork precisely beside his plate and got up to investigate. When he looked out he saw the body of Jim Stacey sprawled face up on the boardwalk about 200 yards away with a group of men and women gawping down at it.

He immediately thought of his wife Marie and looked across Main Street towards Madame Renoir's.

Marie was in Madame Renoir's emporium trying on hats when she heard the shot.

'So your boy Tom is coming in on the stage,' Madame Renoir was saying. 'He's a fine brainy boy, that one.'

'He wants to be a lawyer,' Marie said. 'He should go

13

East to study. That's what Tom and I aim for. But Tom junior is conscientious. Feels he's not yet ready to cut loose from the ranch.'

'But you got Jason, don't you? He'll make a fine rancher in his time. Every man and woman has his own niche in the world, you know, Mrs Flint.'

Madame Renoir and Marie Flint were a good matching pair in matronly dignity. Madame Renoir had something attractively French in her accent, which she cultivated, and she held herself like a queen. Marie Flint was more than queenly; though well advanced in years she had a natural regality about her and it was obvious she had been a beauty in her day. She and Tom Flint had ridden West in sixty-two, as the war was raging. At that time they had very little between them, but now in New Mexico they had a good spread with a large herd of longhorns – not as a large as Chisum's, but large enough to be respected in the county and through the New Mexico Territory.

As she was paying for her fine new hat Marie heard the shot.

'Someone's shooting down there!' She went to the door and saw Jim Stacey lying dead on the boardwalk.

'Looks like they killed a man!' Madame Renoir said, standing behind her.

Marie looked across the street and saw Tom her husband emerging from Frenchy's diner. Thank God he's safe! she thought. She remembered the fall of sixty-one when her husband had almost died at the hands of the gunman called Wolf. All that trouble and bloodshed, she thought. We don't want it here in El Jango.

14

Flint stepped off the broadwalk and they met halfway across the street.

'Thank God you're safe!' she said.

They walked down Main Street to where the crowd was gathering round the body of the unfortunate victim. The mayor was still flapping around beside Stacey's body.

'There's two men killed here!' he said. 'How come you were locked in your jail, Cassidy? It's your job to protect this community from such criminals!'

Sheriff Cassidy was wringing his hands and his face had turned purple with shame. 'I couldn't help it. The guy just came into the office, held a gun on me, and locked me in my own jail.'

Nobody had the indecency to laugh. With two men lying dead and their widows to consider it was hardly a time for mirth.

'What exactly happened?' Pike Willcox demanded. He had a pencil in one hand and his pad in the other. He was the local representative of the *Las Vegas Gazette* and he guessed he had a scoop here. Pity his newfangled camera was in the studio: he could have taken pictures of the bodies; everyone liked to see pictures of corpses, preferably dead villains lying in the street!

The bank manager spilled out a graphic account of the shooting in a bank and told how the bank-robbers must have made off with $10,000, maybe $20,000 at least. The adrenaline was still flowing strong in his veins and he couldn't stop jabbering.

Baldy Barlow slid up beside Tom Flint and said: 'I seed the whole thing, Mr Flint. One of them went into

15

the sheriff's office, four of them went into the bank, and one of them waited outside with the horses. She was a woman.' Though Baldy spoke in a slurred voice and most people didn't take him seriously, Flint was listening intently.

'You say one was a woman?' he said. 'You sure about that?'

'Sure was a woman,' Baldy said. 'I seed her good. I seed the whole thing. All dressed in black with bandannas like covering their faces.'

The mayor turned from Cassidy and started to take an interest. 'A woman, you say? How do you know it was a woman?'

Baldy lurched to one side and twisted his mouth in a grin. 'I knowd it was a woman. I know a woman when I see one, Mr Mayor, even if she is wearing a bandanna over her face.'

Despite the tragedy this gave rise to a titter of laughter.

Cassidy was pulling himself together. 'I should get after those killers,' he said resolutely. He looked round quickly, hoping for some response, but nobody seemed inclined to volunteer to form a posse, especially after the killings.

'I'd come if I could,' Baldy said. 'Mr Stacey was my friend. He was a good man. He gave me twenty-five cents when I paid heed to his stories about the war.'

'They were both good men.' The mayor waved his hand dismissively.

'You can't go,' Marie said to Tom Flint. 'Your days of

16

shooting are over. And the stage is due in in less than an hour. We've got to be here to greet Tom junior.'

Both of these observations were true. In the old days Flint had been known among the Comanche and among his fellow Rangers as *Man of Blood*, but at sixty he had put all that behind him to become a peaceable rancher . . . or so he thought.

Now the funeral director had arrived with his assistant. They lifted the body of Jim Stacey and placed it none too gently in a coffin they had provided. As they went into the bank to pick up Jerry Todd's body from behind the counter, the crowd began to disperse, chattering with amazement and horror.

Cassidy unhitched his horse, strapped his pistol on to his thigh and slid his Winchester into its sheath. He rode off in the direction he had been told the bank-robbers had taken.

Chisum appeared, picking morsels of steak out of his teeth with a toothpick. 'That boy hasn't a hope in hell of tracking those criminals,' he announced contemptuously. 'And what's he aim to do when he finds them? A silver badge won't make those bank-robbers lie down and lick their tails.'

'You could be right,' Flint said.

'He hasn't the savvy to run down a grasshopper,' Chisum continued. 'What do you think to that story he got himself locked in his own cell?'

Marie and Tom exchanged glances.

'What do you think?' Marie said.

'Pardon my language, ma'am,' Chisum said, 'but I think that could be a load of old bullshit.'

17

'Are you saying he locked himself in?' Flint suggested with irony.

Chisum paused to pick his teeth and consider. 'Could be,' he said. 'That young Cassidy might not have the balls on him to face up to killers like that but he has enough savvy to lock himself in his own cell and throw the key out!'

Marie's eyes were popping. 'They say he did some brave things down south of here, Mr Chisum. We hear he foiled a robbery down there.'

Chisum wrinkled his warty nose. 'Maybe he did and maybe he didn't. I'm just saying I don't feel right about that boy. He's not the kind to make a good lawman. Wouldn't survive in a town like Abilene or Dodge City. That's all I'm saying.' He nodded at Marie. 'By the way, Mrs Flint, I do admire your new hat. It's real purty.'

CHAPTER TWO

Cassidy hadn't a hope in Hades of catching the six bank-robbers. His riding skills were no more then average and he sat his horse like a travelling preacher or an aspiring lawyer which, among other things, he was. When it came to tracking he was no Apache Indian. But it wasn't as difficult as he had expected to pick up the trail of the six riders.

Yet Cassidy had no real intention of coming up with the six riders even if he could. Thoughts of a shoot-out didn't worry him too much. After all, hadn't he been shooting at bottles and cans in the yard behind the office for the last six months? He knew he could shoot straight and fast in normal circumstances. But these circumstances were far from normal. He was still feeling sore about the whole damned business – sore and guilty: guilty because two innocent men had been gunned down in cold blood while he was locked in his own jail. He felt particularly bad about the death of Jim Stacey, who had befriended him and encouraged him, and Jerry Todd had never harmed a soul. He didn't even swat down flies in the office. And Cassidy felt guilty because he had been party to a scam. More than that: he had been made to look as big a fool as Baldy Barlow. Like Tom Flint junior, Tom Flint's son who was studying the law, he had a hankering to train for the law. Serving as sheriff might make him respectable, but now this damned fool thing had occurred and he had gambled his future away at the throw of a dice. And the dice had come up with the big six of love. Or so he had thought.

As he rode on, he felt furious with himself. What the hell am I doing out here on my own? he thought. Why didn't I stay back there and get a posse together before I rode out on this fool's errand? He knew he couldn't have expected Tom Flint or John Chisum to join a posse. Chisum sneered at everything he did and Flint had ridden into town to pick up his son Tom junior coming in on the stage from Santa Fe. And, anyway, both of them were too old to go rousting round the county looking for criminals and risking getting shot.

Yet, as he rode along looking for sign, he knew he was on the right track. The bank-robbers were headed in the direction of the Pecos. A wise decision, since, after they crossed the river, it would be near impossible to pick up their trail.

Out of the heat haze he saw a wagon looming towards him, drawn by a couple of mangy burros. Three Mexicans: a man with a grizzled beard at the reins, a woman walking behind, trailing a half-starved kid – probably a girl in the ragged clothes of a boy.

As he approached the man pulled on his reins and the rig drew to a halt.

'You seen a bunch of riders?' Cassidy asked him.

'*Sí señor*. We see them,' the Mexican sang out confidently. 'They ride that way.' He jerked his thumb over his shoulder. 'Ride pretty damned fast too.'

'How many?' Cassidy asked.

The Mexican shrugged his shoulders. 'Many,' he said. 'Maybe six, seven.' He grinned and nodded his head encouragingly. 'They got bandannas covering their faces like they don't want to be recognized.'

'Six of them. They shoot their guns!' The girl who was dressed as a boy suddenly piped up. 'Pow! pow!' Pretending to hold an invisible pistol.

'They shoot at you?' Cassidy asked.

The Mexican and the woman glanced at one another uneasily.

'No, *señor*. They shoot in the air. They laugh and shoot like they gone crazy.'

'Thank you.' Cassidy pricked his mount with his spurs and rode on. Shooting off at random wasn't good. It could be those bank-robbers were high on peyote or something which could make them highly unpredictable. That was something he hadn't taken into account. Peyote could make a man see visions or go crazy. The Apaches knew how to use it, but, in the hands of white fools, it might lead to anything!

It was a damned sight too hot for riding. He should turn back and bide his time and, maybe, hire an Apache scout or something. Yet he rode on with the imaginary laughter of men like Chisum and Joe Slocum, the mayor, cackling in his imagination.

Fear and guilt came in waves like the shimmering

21

light striking up from the desert. And then he saw what looked like a phantom riding towards him: the stage coming down from Santa Fe.

As he approached the stage a strange uneasiness gripped at his throat. There was something wrong with the picture. Instead of bowling along on the last miles of its journey towards El Jango, the stage sat dead still and people were gathering round it like flies round a dead horse or a pile of dung. Something had clearly gone very wrong!

At the depot in El Jango Tom Flint consulted his fob watch. 'Stage is late. Should have been here an hour back.'

It wasn't unusual for the stage to be late. Running on time was difficult. There were so many variables. Sometimes a wheel bust or there was a flash flood. There were places where the stage could hole up and wait for the weather to improve. But on this occasion the weather was good though almost unbearably hot. Flint felt far from easy and he saw that Marie was getting decidedly fidgety, waiting to welcome her elder boy.

When at last the stage came into view nobody shouted or cheered. Each man and woman was straining forward and trying to figure what might have caused the delay. Everyone was on tenterhooks because of the recent bank bust.

'That's Cassidy!' Mayor Slocum said. 'Looks like he's riding shotgun. Or maybe he's changed his mind and turned back.'

The stage rolled in slowly and pulled up beside the depot. The disembarking passengers looked solemn and terrified like they'd had the guts knocked out of them.

'What happened?' Chisum shouted.

Cassidy looked down from his mount. Flint saw that he appeared to be no more than a boy pretending to be a man, but the expression on the sheriff's face worried him. 'They got Tom junior,' Cassidy said. His face was as white as a sheet drying in the wind.

'What d'you mean, got him?' Flint asked. His voice came out hoarse. The last passengers were clear of the stage and there was no sign of his son Tom.

'What happened to Tom?' Marie gasped with her hand up to her mouth.

Cassidy shook his head. He seemed too shocked to speak.

The driver, an older, deeply experienced man, filled in. 'Those desperadoes rode off with young Flint. They beat up on him and took him off like he was a hostage or something.'

'Oh, my God!' cried Marie.

Flint pieced the story together from what the stage driver and the passengers told him.

The stage had been driving along nice and easy, looking forward to getting in on time. It was too hot for comfort and the women were fanning themselves with their kerchiefs. but they would soon be pulling in at the depot where they could relax, take a cold drink, go home, or book up for the night in the hotel. For some time nobody had said much, but now, at the thought of arrival, conversation had revived somewhat. People were chatting about the friends and relations who would be waiting for them or about the deals they hoped to pull off when they reached El Jango.

'That young man was real quiet and dignified,' a lady said, referring to Tom Flint junior. 'He was obviously a scholar and he kept himself to himself.'

' 'Cept when those desperadoes came rampaging in,' said the driver. 'Then he said a few things.'

'A few things they didn't like,' another man agreed solemnly.

It seemed that the five men and one woman – yes, there was definitely a woman among them, quite young and not a bad-looker – came riding in and around the passengers like the thing was just one bunch of laughter. Everyone on the stage thought there was a fun day or some celebration in El Jango, until those scum drew guns and started firing them off every which ways.

Then they made all the passengers get out of the coach, stand in line like army recruits, and give up what valuables they possessed, money and watches from the men, necklaces and diamond rings from the women. There was a deal of screaming and complaining but the only person who spoke out against the robbery was Tom Flint junior.

'He was so riled up, he'd have taken a shot at those desperate men if he'd been armed!' the driver shouted. 'But he didn't get a chance. One of those desperadoes rode right up to him and beat him about the head with a pistol. Never seen anyone beat up on a man so revengeful in my life!'

'There was a lot of blood!' a woman screamed.

'There was that!' the driver agreed. 'But that brave young man just sneezed out blood and raised his head good and brave.

'And one of those desperate men – the leader I guess he was – said: "Is your name Flint by any chance?"

' "He's a Flint," another of those desperadoes said.
' "I seen him before. Son of Tom Flint, your dad's old buddy, Randy," one of the others roared.

' "Shut your mouth!" the leader of the bunch shouted. "You Tom Flint's son?" he asked Tom Flint junior.

'They lifted the brave young man's head and the man called Randy stared right into his eyes. "You're Tom Flint junior for sure," he said.

'Then he pushed young Tom's head back hard, as if he wanted to snap it off.

'The young woman in the party tried to put a stop to the things they did, but they just roped Tom up like a steer. They forced him to mount up on a spare horse they had, and they rode off with him drooping sideways as though he was ready to fall.'

These graphic details did nothing to allay Marie Flint's fears. She had her hand up to her face to conceal it from the onlookers and she was shuddering with the grief and horror of what had happened to her son. Marie was a woman who had stood up to much hardship and looked into the face of death many times and she didn't care to show her emotions.

Flint put his arm round her shoulders and took her

into the depot so she could recover somewhat from the shock.

John Chisum came and stood beside him. Flint and Chisum had never exactly liked one another, but because they were both ranchers they shared a kind of mutual respect.

'What do you aim to do?' Chisum asked.

Flint had the kind of look on his face he had had when the gunslinger Wolf had tried to kill him all those years before. His eyes had narrowed, his face had grown deadly pale, and his jaw was set. 'Someone lend me a gun and a riding-horse, I'll go after those mad *pistoleros* and shoot them down like the rats they are,' he murmured almost inaudibly.

'I'll ride with you,' Chisum declared.

'I'll come too,' Sheriff Cassidy said. 'That's my job.'

The young woman in the party tried to put a stop to the things they did, Flint remembered them saying. It gave him a small crumb of comfort.

After a moment's hesitation one or two other men were shamed into riding along too.

They rode out along the stagecoach trail until they reached the place where it had been forced to stop. Nobody said much. Flint was slightly ahead. He held up his hand and the bunch of them reined in. Flint was greatly respected, not only because he was a rancher of some consequence but because of his reputation from the time he was a Ranger and the name *Man of Blood* the Comanches had pinned on him. Flint was no Indian tracker but he knew how to read the signs. After he had studied the horse tracks, he dismounted and bent to look at them more closely.

Cassidy was surprised at how cool and calculating Flint appeared to be despite the fact that Tom junior had been beaten up badly and was missing. Cassidy was upset, not only because of his own perceived failure and guilt, but because Tom junior had been a friend of many years. For him this was the worst betrayal. He watched, fascinated, as Flint remounted and peered off into the heat haze. Flint raised his arm like a captain of cavalry ordering an advance and the small cavalcade rode on in silence.

But not for long. A few miles along on the trail they found what they were looking for and what they had dreaded – a man tied to a mesquite tree. The man, scarcely recognizable from the blood covering his face, was Tom Flint junior. He was tied to the mesquite tree like a crucified Christ.

Flint dismounted with slow deliberation and examined his son closely, but he knew already that Tom junior was dead.

My God, that man has a spike of ice in his heart, Cassidy thought as Flint turned and stared at Chisum.

'I'm sorry, Flint. That's too bad,' Chisum said solemnly.

Flint shook his head slowly, as though he was remembering something from way back in the past.

The rest of the crew groaned quietly. Almost all of them knew the studious young man who was intent on studying the law.

Battered to death by monsters, Cassidy thought. His

27

feeling of guilt grew to a point like an invisible nail in his heart. He could hardly breathe, especially when he thought of the woman. Yet he remembered again the words *The young woman in the party tried to put a stop to the things they did.* Though now there seemed no comfort in them.

They untangled Tom junior's body from the mesquite tree and laid it gently on the ground. Chisum was reading from a scrap of paper that had been stuffed into the pocket of the dead man.

It said: *Keep out of our hair all would-be lawmen unless you want yours.* Underneath was scrawled the words: *The Regulators.*

This applies specially to skunks with the name of Flint!

They rolled Tom Flint junior's body in a poncho that someone had offered and Flint and Chisum conferred.

'Seems this is a personal vendetta. What do we do now?' Chisum asked Flint.

Flint looked Chisum in the eye, straight and calculating. 'I want for you to ride back and talk to Marie. Tell her what happened as gently as you can. Don't let her see the body before it gets cleaned up. The rest of you men take my son in. Mr Cassidy, I want you to take charge of that part.'

'What do you aim to do?' Cassidy asked him.

Flint gave him a strange look, as though he was amazed that he could have asked such a damned fool question. 'I'm going after those killers,' he said.

This gave Cassidy a chance to redeem himself a little. 'You go after them, I come too,' he said.

Flint nodded grimly. He had half-expected Cassidy's answer and, despite his growing suspicions, he respected the boy's apparent determination.

'If the rest of you boys would kindly ride back with Mr Chisum I'd appreciate it.'

One of the bolder men said: 'You catch up with those killers, that's two against six. You could be gunned down too.'

'I don't think so,' Flint said. 'Not if you lend me that shooter of yours.' He had ridden into El Jango on the buckboard without his Colt Peacemaker, though he had grabbed his Winchester after the stage came in.

The man who had spoken solemnly handed over his shooter. 'Good luck, Mr Flint.'

Flint and Cassidy rode on, following the signs on the trail.

'What happens when we catch up with them?' Cassidy asked.

Flint stared straight ahead. 'I want to thank you for riding with me,' he said. It's a pity they locked you in the jail. You shouldn't let yourself feel too bad about that.'

'Thank you, Mr Flint,' the young man said.

'But if you expect to see more bloodshed today,' Flint continued, 'I think you're in for another disappointment.'

'Why would that be?'

Flint was still looking ahead into the haze. 'They may be high on something but not high enough to forget to cover their tracks. They're not going to the Pecos all bunched up to give us an easy target. They'll split up and go on in their own ways. Meet up later, probably after they cross the river.'

'Not much sense in following one of them,' Cassidy said. 'When they hit the Pecos we lose them anyway.'

'That's the truth of it,' Flint agreed.

They reached the parting of the ways quite soon. Flint got down from his horse and studied the hoof-marks. 'This is the break-up point,' he said. 'The devil woman went that way.' He pointed right into an area covered with chaparral.

'How did you know that?' Cassidy marvelled.

'I put two and two together and came up with five,' Flint said grimly. 'You see this hoof-mark. Nail missing. Saw it back where they attacked the stage where they pistol-whipped my boy and again by the mesquite where they strung him up. That's my hunch and I'm sticking with it.' He straightened up. 'That woman must be a demon from hell.'

Cassidy had turned as pale as parchment. For a moment he could hardly catch his breath. He remembered the words again: *The young woman in the party tried to put a stop to the things they did,* but now they were even less comforting.

'What do we do now?' he asked.

Flint nodded. 'We go back. I look after Marie in her grieving.' He gritted his teeth. 'And we do a little more detective work. See if we can pin-point those hell-hounds.'

CHAPTER THREE

They buried Tom Flint junior in the burial ground close to the town. It was a neat patch of land on a bluff just beyond the town limits. The Reverend Theo Jenkins had a particular talent for funerals and Marie thought he was a good man. She was still in denial and couldn't get her head round the fact that her elder son who was destined for the law and could even go as far as the senate was dead and killed in such a brutal manner.

Flint hadn't so far mentioned the fateful message tucked into his son's pocket: *Keep out of our hair all would-be lawmen unless you want yours.* Underneath scrawled the words: *The Regulators.*

This applies specially to skunks with the name of Flint!

Flint seemed strangely composed and thoughtful through the funeral. Nobody would have seen the extent of his suffering. But it was a hard and bitter frontier and he had seen many men die by violence, including his brother Hank, butchered by thugs pretending to be Cherokee Indians.

Chisum came, looking old but smart in his best Sunday-going suit. After the funeral he drew Flint aside. 'What's our next move?' he asked.

Flint turned to look at him gravely. 'I appreciate the question, John, and I'm still looking for the answer.'

'Have you thought on Cassidy?' Chisum said. He was a man who cherished suspicion, especially after all that had happened in the recent Lincoln County range war.

'Cassidy is just a boy with a star on his vest,' Flint said.

'Maybe you should look at him a bit closer,' Chisum suggested. He shook his head and looked like a polecat in a particularly ornery mood. 'I've been thinking about matters, particularly what happened last year.'

Flint took notice. 'Sure. You mean with Pat Garrett shooting the Kid down in Fort Sumner?'

Chisum glanced away. Despite the fact that he was glad to be rid of William Bonney, alias Billy the Kid, he felt somewhat guilty about the way the Kid had died, shot down in cold blood in Pete Maxwell's bedroom by Pat Garrett. Nobody likes to see a man shot down without a fight. Even a killer like the Kid needs a fair chance before he dies.

'I've been thinking on that note they stuffed into Tom junior's pocket,' he added. 'Remember what they wrote: *Keep out of our hair all would-be lawmen unless you want yours.* It was signed: *The Regulators.* And then there was that bit at the end: *Especially if your name's Flint!* Have you thought about what that might mean?'

'I've thought about it all the time,' Flint said. 'Something from the past trying to trade down on me. Should have been me on the stage and not an innocent young man like Tom junior.'

'And what do you think about The Regulators?' Chisum asked.

Flint was way ahead of Chisum on that one. In the Lincoln County War, which had ended more or less with the Kid's death, the so-called Regulators had set themselves up because they figured the lawmakers were corrupt. So there could be some kind of connection there. If so, why did they pick El Jango, probably the most peaceable town in New Mexico? And why hadn't they shot down Sheriff Cassidy instead of locking him in his own cell? And what was the connection between the Flints and the Lincoln County War? Or was that a separate tea kettle altogether?

Though Flint was allied to John Chisum in so far as he was a neighbouring rancher, he had kept himself clear of the range war and had had no dealings with the Kid or with Pat Garrett.

'I don't figure it,' he said. 'Those Regulators might have done a lot of killing but they were driven by a principle. These men – and the woman – are driven by greed and bloodlust and possibly by peyote. That's why we have to stop them.'

'Don't forget the revenge angle,' Chisum reminded him. 'Is that part of the deal?'

That's a damned fool thing to ask, Flint thought. 'I'm still working on that,' he said.

'And the peyote,' Chisum added.

'Man or woman takes peyote, he's asking for a heap of trouble,' Flint agreed.

Both men knew about peyote, the cactus drug the

33

Apache used to induce a trancelike state and visions of another world but which could also send a man into a frenzy of violence.

'Either way, these killers need to be shot down like rabid dogs,' Chisum egged on.

Flint kept silence for a moment.

'If we knew where to find them, or who they are,' he said grimly. 'One of the stage passengers mentioned the leader of the gang was called Randy. You know anybody by the name of Randy or Randolph?'

'Can't say it's a name I've come across too frequently,' Chisum said. 'Sounds a little fancy to me. Worth remembering though. Could be an important lead.' He stroked his moustaches down flat for a second. 'And one of them was a woman too. That's another clue.'

The idea of a woman being in on the killing of Tom junior seemed to add to the injustice. Flint had encountered a good many hard women in his time but the thought of a good-looking woman being complicit in Tom's pistol-whipping and murder seemed more than usually outrageous.

But now his attention was drawn to Baldy Barlow who had cried like a child all through the funeral proceedings and then had had a fit.

'That damned idiot would do anything to attract attention to himself,' Mayor Joe Slocum said in disgust.

Reverend Theo Jenkins was heard to mutter that Baldy could be possessed by the Devil and might need to be exorcised.

*

Pike Willcox, the local reporter, had sent his article to the *Las Vegas Gazette* and the editor had given it a good spread with grainy photos of the bank and an interview with the manager, who was strutting round town boasting that he had only just managed to dodge out of the way of the bank-robbers' bullets. Lew Wallace, the governor, sent a message of condolence, said he would have liked to do something but was on the point of retiring: he had his book *Ben Hur* about a Roman slave to write. Sheriff Cassidy had called in the deputy marshal who promised to do what he could – which didn't amount to row of beans. Cassidy had also put up posters around the town under the heading *Wanted Dead or Alive* and the town elders had offered a modest reward for the apprehension of the killers and bank-robbers.

But nothing happened. El Jango settled once again into a midsummer torpor.

Yet things were not the same and things would never be the same. Sheriff Cassidy gnawed on his teeth with apparent mortification and kept his six-gun strapped to his thigh at all times. They said he slept with it under his pillow every night, which might have been inconvenient if he had been married. When he did his accounts in the office or locked a drunk in the cells he kept the door of the office secure, so anybody wanting admittance had to knock three times and shout and show himself at the window He had a good idea that Chisum and a few others thought he was at best weak-kneed, and at worst the most ineffective and guilty sheriff in the territory.

The mayor, Joe Slocum, was a useless old geek so swollen with his own pride you couldn't talk anything through with him. But Cassidy needed to talk. He had thought of talking to Flint – in fact, he badly wanted to – but hardly knew how to approach him. Flint had become strangely distant. Mostly he kept out of town and after the funeral he concentrated on the doings of the ranch. It would soon be round-up time and another drive along the Goodnight-Loving trail to Cimmaron and Cheyenne was in the offing.

Flint also had to keep a watchful eye on his second son, Jason. Jason was different again from Tom junior. There was no scholar in him. He was all for the range and for a life of action. He seemed tough as rawhide. Very much a younger Tom Flint but bigger and beefier. Jason favoured his mother for looks and she had been a fine-looking woman in her day.

The shock of Tom junior's death was like a tornado hitting Jason. Though they were very different in temperament the two brothers had been very close. Jason had looked up to his elder brother and now he couldn't believe he had gone.

'What do we do about this thing?' Jason demanded of his father.

'What we do about this is we wait,' Flint said unconvincingly.

'How wait?' Jason shouted. 'We wait nothing happens. You want things to happen you got to make them happen!' He couldn't understand his father's patience. Doing nothing was just weakness. Hadn't Flint once been an Indian fighter? Hadn't he earned the name Man of Blood from the Comanches? What had happened to him since those days? Where had his balls gone? Had they shrivelled away and left him a coward?

'We make things happen when we know how to make things happen,' Flint said.

And things did happen and sooner than either of them expected.

Jason had reached the point when he couldn't keep still because of his grieving and his exasperation. About a week after the bank hold-up and the killings he rode out to the perimeter of the ranch and caught two Mexicans riding off a couple of the steers. Two of the boys from the spread brought them in with the steers. They had tied up the Mexicans. One was an older man about forty. He was bald and had yellowish features made paler with fear, and little beads of sweat had broken out all over his forehead. The younger one was just a kid, no more than twelve, or maybe a stunted fifteen.

'You see these two steers?' Jason shouted down at them from his horse.

'We see them, *señor*,' the man said, trembling with terror.

'You happen to see the brands?' Jason bawled at him.

The Mexican had no reply: anyone could see the brand – a double S with three slashes cut through like a dollar sign.

'You steal these two steers?' Jason accused.

'No, *señor*. We see them. We not steal them. We bring them back to you.' He was sweating so much one of the boys took a bandanna and wiped his brow.

Jason dismounted slowly. 'You know what happens to cattle-thieves around here?'

The Mexican shook his head and swallowed hard like he had a prickly pear stuck in his gullet.

Jason swung to concentrate on the boy. 'You steal these steers?' he accused.

The boy seemed much more courageous than his father. Maybe he didn't know the penalty for stealing cattle. He spoke up bravely: 'No, *señor.*'

Jason strutted around him, exasperated. 'What d'you mean, *no?* You know what we do out here to people who steal cattle?'

There was a deadly silence. The Mexican boy looked at the ground. One of the Slashed S outfit was playing out his lariat, ready to throw over a branch of a dead tree. The tree had the sinister look of a rotting man holding his arms outstretched as if asking the question *why did this happen to me?*

'Please, *señor,*' the Mexican begged. 'We poor. We have nothing. You turn us loose, we don't come back.'

The lariat was now over the dead tree. The cowpuncher who had hurled over the branch of the dead tree pulled on it to test the strength of the branch and the rope swung with the loop dangling ready. One of the boys heaved another rope up so that the two loops swung side by side, waiting to be drawn over the heads of the two Mexicans.

The men of the Slashed S looked up to Jason, He had proved himself to be one of them. He seemed tough as hell but, though he was hasty and quick to anger, he wasn't a violent man. He had to brazen it out to show who was the boss. He had never seen a man swing before, let alone a boy, but he knew it was his responsibility and the men were watching him, some with uneasiness in their eyes, others with bloodlust in their expressions, especially Steve Rollins a veteran of the war, for whom life and death were cheap and who despised Mexicans and Indians and any sign of weakness in other men.

'Let's get this over with,' Steve Rollins said. 'These greasy Mexes make me sick to my stomach.'

The boys grabbed the trembling Mexican and heaved him up on to a horse. They seized the boy who weighed no more than a small bag of hay and heaved him up on to another horse. Then they looped the lariats over their heads. and pulled them tight so their tongues hung out. The man started praying and the boy stared straight out as if making up his mind to die bravely, though there was panic in his eyes.

'Please, *señor*,' the man choked out. against the rope. 'Let my son go! He is innocent boy! I take the blame! Let him go!'

The Slashed S boys were looking at Jason, studying him close, waiting for him to give the word. The two horses were treading the ground, ready and eager to gallop.

'Please, *señor*!' the Mexican pleaded. 'He is a boy! Please save my son!'

The boy clenched his jaw and started to mumble a prayer. Even Steve Rollins could see he was a boy with real sand. But the *eye for an eye* law of the range stood and the kid had to die.

Jason sat in the saddle. He was trying to make up his mind to give the order. There could be no turning back now unless he wanted to make himself look a damned fool and lose all authority with the boys.

As he raised his hand to give the order, a voice came from nowhere: 'Hold on there!'

It was his father Tom Flint who spoke. He had ridden in by another route. He could have stayed in the ranch house or ridden out in another direction. Like his son Jason he had difficulty in keeping still while he was thinking and grieving over Tom junior. When he saw the lynching party, the man and the boy about to swing from the dead tree, he acted from a kind of instinct he couldn't explain.

He rode down to join the lynching party and looked up at the boy about to swing and choke his life out on the dead tree.

'Take the noose off the boy's neck,' he said quietly.

Nobody moved. Even Steve Rollins kept still. One of the cowpunchers sidled up and loosened the rope and lifted it off the boy's head. It was Chuck Little – they called him *Little Chuck* He was the man who had smoothed the sweat off the Mexican's brow with a bandanna. Most of the other men thought he was too soft to be in the cow business.

Nevertheless, some of the boys murmured with relief.

The Mexican boy had turned the colour of a mouldy cheese. He looked as though he would throw up.

'Get the boy down from the horse,' Flint said. He tried not to look at Jason because he knew Jason would think he was undermining his authority with the hands, though everyone knew Flint was the real boss.

'What about this Mexican *hombre*?' Rollins sneered. 'He's the one who did the stealing. The kid's only his sidekick.' Everyone understood that Rollins had a talent for mischief-making and he hated Mexicans. The horrors of the war had given him a taste for blood.

Flint looked at Jason. Jason nodded and spoke up strongly. 'Take the noose off the peon's head!'

Chuck Little took the noose off the man's head. The Mexican started to blubber with relief and terror. A faint jeer rippled among the cowpunchers. Flint had always been amazed by how a man could stand by and enjoy mindless cruelty.

'What do we do now?' Rollins asked.

That was the big question. Flint was about to make a pronouncement, he didn't know what. He could have turned the two of them loose, knowing they might think he was a soft touch, or he could have invented some kind of cruel punishment to please Steve Rollins.

As he looked down at the quivering Mexican there was another intervention. An old quavering voice rose up from among the chaparral and a man who looked like a resurrected Confucius rode out on a burro. He was giving them a toothless grin more out of fear than out of greeting.

'You men,' he cried squeakily. 'You, Mr Flint, I know you.' He urged the mule forward and came among the group. He looked as ridiculous as Sancho Panza might have looked riding his donkey. He stared with rheumy eyes up at Flint. 'Mr Flint, you save my son and my grandson. They good boys. Both are good boys.' He gasped and grabbed air and then turned towards Jason. 'You, the other Señor Flint, I know you too. You good man. You save my son, my grandson. God will reward you.'

He urged his burro forward until he was right below Tom Flint.

'I reward you too,' he said in a quieter, man-to-man voice. 'I tell you something you like to hear.' He looked round slowly at Chuck Little and Steve Rollins and the other men. 'Please, *señor*, this is very dangerous. I do not talk in front of these men. This is for you to hear only. I talk to you alone.'

Flint had what he could only describe later as a premonition. 'OK, boys, turn the man and the boy loose and move off.'

Steve Rollins's mouth dropped open in surprise but he said nothing.

Chuck Little and another man untied the Mexican man and the boy and turned them loose. The boy threw up beside the dead tree. The man bent over to comfort him. They both moved away to where their burro was grazing on what grass it could find.

The Slashed S boys moved off and bunched together, watching Flint with curiosity as he dismounted and stood close to the old grandfather. Jason was still on his horse standing close.

'What have you to tell me, old man?' Flint asked hoarsely.

The old Mexican ran his tongue over his parched lips. 'Señor Flint,' he said quietly, 'I tell you who killed your son.'

Flint rested his hand on the burro's rump. 'You know who killed my son?' he said sceptically.

The old man nodded and looked like a frightened scarecrow. He glanced towards the men bunched up close and then towards the chaparral as though he suspected someone might creep out from behind a bush and shoot him dead. 'I know the man,' he half-whispered.

Flint narrowed his eyes with suspicion. He thought, these people will tell you anything to save their butts, anything they can to please you. Yet, somehow, the old man was different, and now his wizened face creased in a smile.

'How do you know the man?' Flint asked. He felt Jason move close by, with impatience.

Now the old man seemed to gain confidence. 'I know all those men . . .' he paused and licked his dry lips . . . 'and I know that woman too.'

Flint glanced at Jason and saw he understood. How could the old man know about the woman? Maybe the *Las Vegas Gazette* had mentioned a woman but he couldn't be sure.

Flint leaned towards the old man. 'How do you know?'

The old man grabbed the air again. For himself he had nothing to lose; he was almost as old as Methuselah. 'I see what happened to your son,' he gasped. 'I standing close by. Nobody see me. I standing close when they ride past, the five men and the woman. I see them all very much and I know them.'

Jason edged closer. 'You know them,' he said. 'Can

you name them?'

The old man switched to Jason. 'I give you the names,' he said. 'I am nobody. I ride away and you don't see me no more.'

'That's the deal,' Flint said. 'You give these names. nobody will ever know.'

The old man looked somewhat more hopeful. 'You promise that, Señor Flint?'

'You have my word on that, old man.'

The old man reached into a leather pouch he had. He passed Flint a scrap of paper.

'*Adios, amigo,*' he said hopefully. He turned his burro and rode away. The man and the boy had partly recovered from their terror. The father raised a wavering hand. '*Adios, amigo,*' he said. 'We not forget this.'

The boy said nothing. He was already thinking about what he would tell his mother about the narrow squeak they had had.

The Slashed S boys watched in amazement as the Mexicans disappeared among the chaparral.

Flint smoothed out the scrap of paper and read the words *Rosa Ramondo* and *Randolph Remarque.*

CHAPTER FOUR

Baldy Barlow was sitting in Madame Renoir's emporium, half-concealed behind a curtain, when he saw Flint ride into town. Though proud, Madame Renoir had a kind heart and she thought being nice to Baldy would gain her a place in heaven just as long as Baldy kept still and didn't show himself when one of her fine ladies came in to buy a dress or a fancy hat. When that happened Baldy would sneak out by the back door and go over to Frenchy's to sit in another back room with a bowl of soup or stew that Frenchy was kind enough to give him. Or he might go home to hang around his mother who stitched clothes for Madame Renoir. Because Baldy had no permanent occupation, apart from looking after his beloved Indian pony, he had plenty of time to observe everything that passed in El Jango . . . even some things that went on behind the scenes which most other people were too busy to notice. He had a close link-up with Pike Willcox, one of the few people in El Jango who didn't regard Baldy as plumb loco. Baldy often fed Willcox useful information about local scandal and Willcox was always discreet about his sources.

But Baldy hadn't been the same since the day of the hold-up. People noticed he slurred his words more and walked with even more of a lurch to one side than usual. Mayor Slocum had been heard to mutter, 'We must get that idiot into an institution somewhere,' but there were no institutions and, anyway, Baldy lived with his mother who cared for him and nourished him as well as she could on her meagre income.

When Baldy saw Flint riding by, Madame Renoir thought he was about to have another fit. He jumped up from his chair, lurched towards the window and waved his arms. Madame Renoir was glad there were no customers in the shop since idiots waving their arms about could be bad for business.

'What in heaven's name is wrong, Baldy?' she cried.

Baldy shook his head and struggled to get his words together. 'That's Mishter Flint riding past!'

Madame Renoir looked out and saw that Baldy was right. Flint was making one of his rare visits to town. It looked as though he was heading for the sheriff's office.

Before Madame Renoir could stop Baldy, he was halfway across the broadwalk, signalling like semaphore with his hands and arms. Flint drew his horse to a stop and then brought it in close to the broadwalk, stooping to attend to Baldy.

'Mishter Flint, sir, I have to talk to you,' Baldy cried.

Flint paused to glance at Madame Renoir's establishment. He saw her peep from behind the curtain and then draw back as though she wanted to dissociate herself from Baldy's antics.

'Sure, Baldy. I'm listening. Where should we talk –

46

right here?' Flint's premonitions were working again and, like Willcox, he had never regarded Baldy as loco, but as a man with an unfortunate affliction and a particular skill at noticing things.

Baldy seemed uncertain whether to speak. He wobbled and lurched and darted frantic glances around, especially in the direction of the sheriff's office. He leaned up towards Flint. 'Come to Ma's place,' he mouthed.

He turned and shambled away towards the shack where his mother lived. Flint figured it would take him a good ten minutes to reach the place, though Baldy could move much faster than you would expect when he was in a hurry.

It was some two hours later when Flint knocked on the door of the sheriff's office. Cassidy looked through the window and let him in.

'Hi, Mr Flint!' the young sheriff said rather over-cheerfully. 'Please come into the office and set yourself down. I'll brew up coffee and we can talk.' Just as though he had expected Flint and was anxious to discuss matters . . . as indeed he was.

Flint noticed Cassidy had a bottle of cheap whiskey on his desk and, from the smell in the office, he figured the sheriff had been hitting it quite hard. Cassidy was wearing his gunbelt with what looked like a Smith & Wesson in the holster.

'I'm tooled up all the time now,' Cassidy informed him. 'You have to be careful around here ever since the hold-up, you know.' Though his voice sounded cheerful and optimistic, Flint noticed it had a false-

47

sounding ring about it.

Flint sat down at the desk and saw that both cells were empty; so there were no witnesses to their conversation. Flint wasn't the man to beat around the bush but he knew how to be cautious. You have to listen and read the signs when you're riding through Comancheria, and the habit had stuck.

'I dropped by to ask you something,' he said. He was watching Cassidy's face which was always lively but now seemed to go blank as though a shutter had been drawn down over it.

'You want to ask me something,' Cassidy said. It wasn't a question, more a statement of fact.

Flint kept his eyes on the sheriff as he spoke. 'A couple of names I want to put before you. Did you ever hear of a Rosa Ramondo and a Randolph Remarque?'

Flint was watching Cassidy's face, particularly the eyes. You can usually tell from a man's eyes when he's about to tell a lie or was wondering what to do next. Cassidy was blinking a lot and his complexion had become decidedly blotchy. 'Rosa who?' he said.

'Ramondo,' Flint said. 'Rosa Ramondo.'

Cassidy half-closed one eye, as though he was checking through a list in his mind. 'Heard the name somewhere,' he bluffed. 'Can't think where. Sounds Mexican. How does this Rosa figure?'

Flint considered for a moment. 'It doesn't exactly figure anywhere. Just a name that came up in conversation I had recently. Thought as sheriff you might have a line on it.'

Cassidy shook his head slowly. 'Nope. Can't remember where I heard it or even if I did hear it.'

Flint didn't press the point. He had heard enough and seen enough to know Cassidy was lying. 'How about Randolph Remarque?' he said. 'Does that name mean anything to you?' He was still watching Cassidy's face, thinking the sheriff was a better barefaced liar than he had expected.

Cassidy went through the process of pretending to think. He's a good actor, Flint figured. That's one thing I have established. The interesting question is, what has he to lie about?

Cassidy's fingers were playing together on the top of the desk. 'I heard the name Remarque,' he admitted. 'Can't remember where though. You think he might have something to do with these killings?'

A frontal attack. Flint was even more impressed. He decided to switch tactics. 'You said the *hombre* who came into the office that day and locked you in the cell was slightly over medium height, was wearing black leathers and had a bandanna over his lower face.'

'That's right.' Cassidy now stared back at Flint though slightly away to the left as though he was picturing the incident over Flint's left shoulder. 'As I remember he was about five ten. That's not too tall.'

'Anything else you remember about this killer?'

Cassidy shook his head slowly. 'We've been through all that. Like I said, he talked real low, like a growling bear. That's all I remember. It all happened so sudden, so quickly.'

Flint gave a faint grin. 'You think his name could have been Randy ... or Randolph like in Randolph

Remarque?' he asked.

He saw Cassidy's fists clench and his knuckles white on the desk. 'How the hell would I know that, Mr Flint?' the sheriff asked.

Flint was grinning, though he was a mile away from being amused. 'Just thought you might have a hunch,' he said.

Cassidy's mouth was working full time as though he was making up his mind to spill something important out. 'Mr Flint,' he said, 'you know what I felt about your son Tom junior.'

Flint shifted his gaze so that he didn't need to look into the sheriff's eyes. 'I do know you looked up to him, thought he was going to have a great future. Everyone thought that.'

The sheriff was silent for a moment. When he spoke it was as though he had something caught in his throat, making it difficult to breathe. 'If I knew who those killers are and where they're likely to be, I'd go after them right now, you know that?'

Flint reached for his hat. He got up. 'I'll remember that, Sheriff,' he said. He paused a moment. 'In the meantime, I suggest you go easy on the booze. Could be bad for a man in your position. Could slow him down when he needs to be quick with a Smith & Wesson.'

Flint closed the door of the sheriff's office and walked across to the hitching rail. He looked down Main Street in both directions, unhitched his horse and rode thoughtfully back through town in the direction of the ranch. He had a strong sense of unfinished business, even of business that hadn't yet started, but he wasn't yet sure how he meant to proceed. Short of drawing a gun and sticking it in the sheriff's mouth, he hadn't made up his mind what to do.

The way back to the ranch went through some quite rocky country with a deal of cactus and scattered boulders, as though a race of warriors had strewn them around in ancient times. Wasn't there some old Apache myth that told the story of those giants? he wondered as he rode through Spiky Gully.

He didn't wonder for a long. Came a shot and the whining of a Winchester bullet ricocheting from the rocks. Far too close, he thought. Intended for him. He was about to slip from the saddle and grab his own gun, when there was another quick shot, so close it whipped the hat from his head.

Now he was in the lee of the horse and the horse had started to buck.

There came a third shot. This time the horse reared up with a whinny of terror, then dropped down and rolled on to its back with its legs striking out at the air. When it crashed down into the dust, dead as a doornail, it almost rolled on to Flint. But, although not as quick as once he had been, Flint was still agile and he managed to spin away to the side of the trail.

He cocked Old Reliable, his Sharps rifle, wriggled into a more convenient position with a degree of cover, and lay still, trying to slow his breath. Whoever it was who had bushwhacked him was no slouch. He or she could shoot and knew how to choose his position. And he must have knowledge of the direction Flint would ride and when he would ride. Now that Flint was without a horse, his would-be assassin might circle and ride down to finish him off. No use lying like a duck on a shooting range, he figured.

He began to slide and wriggle like a snake into an even more advantageous position away from the trail. He tried to picture in his mind how long it might take for his bushwhacker to climb down and retrieve his mount. It might be twenty minutes, or it could be half an hour.

His calculations weren't far out. As he lay, listening and waiting with every pore of his skin, he heard a sound, faint at first but getting gradually closer. He edged up slowly behind a cactus and steadied himself with Old Reliable. He saw a rider approaching stealthily through the chaparral. Hold your breath and wait until he comes right up to the dead horse. Then let him have it!

But the rider was wily. He, or was it a she? decided not to come too close. Obviously saw the horse was dead and Flint was missing. He wasn't going to make himself an easy target. So he turned away and jogged off through the chaparral. Maybe it was work enough for one day!

Flint drew himself up slowly. Could it be the would-be killer wasn't alone, that this was a ruse to draw him out and show himself? He waited for another five minutes and then cautiously approached the dead horse. The bullet had pierced its chest and drilled through its heart. One gasp, a flurry of desperate kicks, and it was dead.

That was intended for me, Flint thought. It was by no means the first time he had been bushwhacked. So his heart scarcely missed a beat. But this bushwhacker had intended to kill. No doubt about that.

He got down on his hunkers to think. First, could he recognize his would-be killer? The answer to that was no. The man – or was it a woman? – was wearing a long leather coat despite the heat, and a wide-brimmed hat. It could be Cassidy but, there again, it could be anyone.

Then Flint considered his next move. He was about halfway between El Jango and his own spread. He could trudge back to El Jango and risk being laughed at, or he could walk on home to add fuel to Jason's mockery. Which would it be? he wondered.

Before calling on Cassidy Flint had ridden to the shack where Baldy Barlow lived with his mother. Flint already knew the mother, a quiet conscientious woman, quite old now, who spent most of her time stitching garments for other women and looking after Baldy. Rachel Barlow's husband, Jonathan, had died about five years earlier in a railroad accident.

Despite Baldy's handicap, Rachel thought the world of her son and she was worried about what would happen to him when she died.

When Flint appeared at the door of the shack Rachel welcomed him in with her usual doleful hospitality, but Flint noticed that she peered out beyond him as though she suspected someone else might be lurking behind the buildings to peek at them.

'Come along in, Mr Flint,' she crowed. 'It's a long sad time since I saw you last.' She went into a considerable profession of grief for Tom junior. 'He was a real good son to you and Marie,' she said,' and I do believe he had a very promising career before him. It's real sad.'

'Thank you, Mrs Barlow,' Flint said tersely. 'I've come to see Baldy. Met him back in town. Said he wanted to tell me something.'

Rachel threw up her hands. 'You don't want to be listening to Baldy!' she said. 'He always has some strange tale to tell. A lot of the time he lives in his dreams, you know.'

'Thash not true, Mother. You know thash not true,' Baldy shouted from an inner room. He came out wearing a blue cravat with big yellow spots to impress Flint. 'Give Mishter Flint a cup of that special drink you brew.'

Flint wondered what that brew could be but he didn't want to embarrass Baldy's mother. 'No need to worry about that,' he said. 'I'll just hear what Baldy has to say to me and then I'll be on my way.'

'You're welcome, Mr Flint,' the lady said, 'but if that's what you want I'll go into my sewing-room and leave you to talk. But mind you, Mr Flint, don't take much heed to my son and the nonsense he talks.'

Mrs Barlow shuffled off into another room at the back and Baldy sat down on a chair. 'Sit you down, Mishter Flint,' he slurred.

Flint sat on the only other chair in the room and leaned forward. 'I hope this is good, Baldy. I don't have much time for gossip.'

'This is no gossip, Mishter Flint. This is the God's truth.'

'OK,' Flint said. 'Fire away, Baldy.'

Baldy rambled on for a while in his usual way which was why people thought he was ten cents short of a dollar, but Flint listened intently and gradually picked out the bones of the story. Apparently Baldy roamed around the town most nights and even sometimes beyond the town limits. Sometimes he went on foot and at other times he rode the Indian pony he loved so much. About half a mile beyond the burial ground there was a ruined shack which had been abandoned by an old miner some years before. It was just a shell: there was nothing much left of it and when kids passed close by they sometimes heard muffled whisperings and groans, which gave rise to the suspicion that it was haunted. Baldy was attracted to hauntings. So he wasn't afraid. *I see things, Mishter Flint, other men don't see.* One night when he was walking off the trail close to the ruin and looking up at the stars, he not only heard something but saw something. From inside the old miner's place there were strange flickerings as though someone had lit a candle. That was no big deal. But on his wanderings through a stand of aspens close to the ruin Baldy had come upon two horses, grazing and hobbled, one of which he recognized.

At this point in the story Flint said nothing. From the way he sat with his eyes half-closed and his elbows resting on the table, you might think he was half-asleep.

Baldy hesitated, it seemed from embarrassment. Then he told how he had crept up to the ruin and listened. He heard two voices talking in low murmurs. One was a man; the other was a woman.

'They seemed a mite more than just friendly,' Baldy sniggered. 'Just like two turtledoves.'

Flint now looked up at him through narrowed eyes.

'Don't get me wrong, Mishter Flint,' Baldy said. 'I

55

wasn't spying nor nothing. I just wondered if they were ghosts but these two were no ghosts, I can tell you.'

Flint nodded. 'You say you recognized one of the horses?'

'Sure I recognized it. I spoke to it quietly and it knew me.'

Flint raised his head a little higher. 'Who owns that horse, Baldy. Can you tell me that?'

Baldy looked deeply embarrassed and nervous. 'I don't want no trouble, Mishter Flint,' he said.

'You won't get trouble from me,' Flint assured him.

'I know you're a man of your word, Mishter Flint, and I trust you. When I got close to the door of that ruin, I heard them moving and I knew they were coming right out. So I got close to a stand of trees and I kept real still. And they came out. Like I said they were like two turtledoves. They went for their horses and I seed them clearly, the man and the woman. The moon was very bright so seeing them was easy.'

Flint drew in a cautious breath. 'Tell me, Baldy, who was the man?'

Baldy hesitated and then came out with it: 'That man was Sheriff Cassidy, Mishter Flint.'

Flint smiled wryly; he wasn't altogether surprised. 'What about the woman. You say you saw her too?'

'Oh, I saw her and I knew her,' Baldy said. 'I seen her before and I never forget a face.'

'Who was that woman, Baldy?' Flint asked.

Baldy twisted his lips in a grin. 'That woman was Rosa Ramondo.'

CHAPTER FIVE

Jason Flint met his father several miles from the ranch. Tom Flint was walking at a good pace along the trail. He had decided to make for the ranch instead of returning to El Jango because he had a lot to think about and he always had his best ideas when he was riding or walking. Also he had a few thoughts he wanted to share with Marie and Jason, though he knew Jason would be champing at the bit for immediate action. Jason was often too headstrong for his own good and, as with hanging the two Mexicans, he sometimes acted before he had given himself time to think.

Uncharacteristically, Jason had been reluctant to ride out and meet Flint, partly because he was still smarting after the episode with the lynching, when he thought his father had made him lose face, and partly because he knew his father was right to spare the poor starving man and the boy.

Yet when he saw Flint trudging along the trail towards him he was surprised. Then he knew he had done the right thing.

Flint showed no sign of relief or pleasure when they met though it was now well on towards evening. Trailing Old Reliable, he looked up at his son and said: 'You'll find a dead horse back there. I'd like to get back to it and get my gear together before the coyotes start ravaging the corpse.'

Jason didn't question his father. He just helped Flint up behind him on his horse and together they rode back along the trail.

When they reached the dead horse, both dismounted and retrieved Flint's saddle, the saddle blanket, and the other gear Flint always carried.

'You been bushwhacked?' Jason said.

'Bushwhacked,' Flint agreed, pointing up at the rocks which were now catching the last rays of the declining sun. 'An *hombre* gunning down on me from up among those rocks.'

'See who did it?' Jason asked.

Flint nodded. 'Saw him, a bit too far off to get a shot in. Wearing a long leather coat and a wide-brimmed Stetson. Could have been anyone, man or woman.'

'A woman!' Jason said. 'You mean it could have been Rosa Ramondo, the woman whose name the Mexicans wrote on the paper?'

'Could have been,' Flint said. 'I didn't get a close look. Whichever way, the bullet was either meant for me or meant to put the scarers on me.'

Jason grunted and they climbed up among the rocks to find the place where the shots had come from. Not too difficult. Flint soon found the signs: a discarded *cigarito* pack and a couple of cartridge cases which Flint collected carefully and stowed away in his breeches pocket. Then they rode back towards the ranch.

When they drew close it was almost dark and they saw lights twinkling out of the ranch house. Marie was on the porch looking plenty worried.

'What happened?' she asked.

'Don't worry,' Flint assured her. 'I survived. I lost a good horse but I survived.'

They went into the house and sat down at table. Marie had already fixed supper and was afraid it might spoil. Jason drained off beer from the keg and they ate a little way apart from the hands, who had already finished their chow and were getting ready to disperse to the bunkhouse.

'Well, why don't you tell us what happened in Spiky Gully?' Jason demanded. He was a terrier and was already straining at the leash though he didn't know which way to jump.

Flint saw that Marie was worried. So he spelled out the whole story, including not only what Baldy had told him and what Cassidy had said to him, but details of the bushwhacking.

'Who would want to do that to you?' Marie asked.

Flint shook his head and said nothing.

Jason burst out: 'If it wasn't the woman, it must have been Cassidy. It's the only answer!'

Flint went on chewing for half a minute. 'I don't know about Cassidy,' he said. 'Why would Cassidy want to do that? He didn't know what Baldy had said to me. He has no reason I figure to want to kill me. And he and Tom junior were good friends at one time.'

Jason shrugged. 'It's the only explanation. I can't see anything else.' He was already starting to boil up. 'Tomorrow come sun-up, we ride in and talk to Cassidy, find out what game he thinks he's playing.' He rose from the table in a boiling rage. 'We lost my brother. We got to find out who did that. Don't you see?'

Flint did see, but at that point not far enough. 'OK, we ride in come sun-up,' he conceded. 'Cassidy might have the key to the big part of this mystery. I guess I need to talk to him.'

'Not without me!' Jason fumed. 'This time I'm coming in with you.'

Flint looked at Marie and Marie raised her eyebrows. He saw she agreed with him; Jason might land them in a heap of trouble with his quick temper. So he nodded slowly. 'Just as long as you let me do the talking. One on one is the best way with a man like Cassidy. If he feels uneasy or put into a corner we get the wrong story.'

Though Jason was somewhat purple around the jowls, he seemed to settle for that.

As it turned out, riding into El Jango proved unnecessary. Next morning while Flint and Jason were saddling up ready to go, Marie came out of the ranch house.

'I think he's here!' she called with her slightly Irish-sounding lilt.

'Who's here?' Jason demanded.

'There's a man riding over the hill! It looks like Cassidy!'

It was Cassidy. Flint saw at once from the way he rode. Not quite as straight and tall in the saddle as a rancher or an Indian but a lot straighter than your average man of the law. Cassidy rode up to the ranch house and held his Stetson out to Marie.

' 'Morning, Mrs Flint,' he said a little over-politely.

Marie knew how to play up to people when she saw the need. ' 'Morning, Mister Cassidy. You're right early. The sun's only just looked over the hill. Please step inside and take a bite of breakfast.'

'Thank you, ma'am. That's real kind.' Cassidy swung down from his horse and looked at Flint. 'I see you were ready to ride, Mr Flint.'

Flint looked him in the eye in his sharp and direct way. 'I thought of riding in to El Jango,' he said. 'We have a few more things to say to one another. I don't think yesterday was enough.'

Cassidy ducked his head with embarrassment. 'That's true, Mr Flint,' he agreed. All this was close to play-acting and Flint knew it. He could see from Jason's expressive face that Jason was thinking: this is the man who helped to kill my brother and we're asking him to take breakfast in the house.

'You have things to share with me, Cassidy?' Jason asked abruptly.

Cassidy looked at Jason and shook his head. 'I thought I'd speak to Mr Flint first,' he said warily. 'Maybe we can talk later when I've said my piece.'

Jason grunted. 'This time you talk to both of us, Cassidy.'

Cassidy thought for a bit. 'OK, it that's the way you want to play it,' he agreed.

They went into the ranch house and Marie discreetly

left them alone. When they were seated over from one another across the table, Flint and Jason on one side and Cassidy on the other, Flint gave Cassidy an opening. 'Someone took a couple of shots at me through Spiky Gully,' he said.

Cassidy looked suitably shocked but Flint had heard him lie before. So he wasn't impressed.

'You mean someone bushwhacked you?' Cassidy said.

Flint grinned in a none-too-amiable manner. 'Shot my horse from under me. Good horse too. It happened as I rode back from town after talking to you.' He drew his hand across his somewhat craggy jaw. 'Occurred to me it could be you.'

The accusation hit Cassidy like a hammer blow to the forehead. He rocked back in his chair and gaped at Flint and then at Jason in astonishment. 'You mean you thought I might have taken a shot at you?' he said. 'I can't believe this! Why would I do a thing like that?' Cassidy's face purpled over. Was it with outrage or guilt? 'You think I rode out here this morning to see if you were dead? Is that what you think?'

Flint paused as Marie brought in a tray of coffee and set it down between them. Cassidy was still struggling to regain his composure when she left them again.

'Why would I take a shot at you, Mr Flint?' he repeated in obvious astonishment. He stared at Jason in bewilderment, but for once Jason kept silent.

'I didn't say you did; I said you might have. Thought it could be because of Rosa Ramondo,' Flint said, looking at Cassidy directly.

Cassidy stared down at his coffee in dismay. 'You mentioned Rosa yesterday,' he said. 'What did you mean by that?'

'I heard one or two things,' Flint admitted. 'Put two and two together. I guess she was the woman tending the horses when those killers robbed the bank.'

Cassidy had now turned from purple to yellow. 'You knew that?' he half-whispered.

'And she was there when they killed my son, Tom junior,' Flint pushed on relentlessly. 'She might even have had more than a small part in that killing.'

Cassidy gulped as though he had a stone suck in the back of his throat. 'That shouldn't have happened,' he said in a hoarse whisper. 'That should never have happened. And that's the reason I had to come to talk to you again.'

'Another thing,' Flint continued. 'I guess Rosa Ramondo is your woman lover. And that's another reason why this mess happened.'

Cassidy opened his eyes in astonishment and then hung his head like a sick dog. For a second he didn't know what to say. 'How come you know these things?' he asked. 'I came to talk to you about all this, and you know half of it already.'

Flint nodded. 'I know half,' he agreed. 'I'm glad you came because now you can tell me the other half – the important half.'

After a moment's hesitation, Cassidy spilled out the whole story.

It was some months earlier. Cassidy was drinking in the

Rio Pecos saloon, a little wayside saloon-cum-small inn down Fort Sumner way. Set up by Steve Wheeler, a big man with a huge belly who boasted constantly about his prowess as an Indian fighter and who claimed to have played a big part in quelling the Navaho with Kit Carson in the Canyon de Chelly in 1863.

Cassidy was impressed by Wheeler's boastful talk at first, but Wheeler was a man whose bragging soon wore thin. While he was talking to Cassidy about the Indian he had scalped, a bunch of riders came into the saloon and started to drink. Among them was a fine-looking Latino woman who talked and horsed around like a man. Cassidy heard them calling her Rose of the South. Her name was Rosa Ramondo.

Rosa drank with the boys like she was one of them. When she saw Cassidy sitting alone, she came over and sidled up to him.

'Hi there, *cabellero*. Can you give me a light for my cigar?'

Cassidy couldn't oblige. He didn't smoke. So Wheeler struck out a flame as big as a gush from a volcano and held it close. Rosa's cigar was no more than a cheroot or a *cigarito* which she acknowledged with a laugh and a flourish.

'You ride in from far?' she enquired, blowing smoke in Cassidy's face.

'I come from El Jango,' he said.

'El Jango, is it?' she said. 'Hey, boys, this *hombre* comes from El Jango way.'

The boys she referred to had lined up on stools at the bar and their heads came round like cows in a stall.

Only these were no cows. They had hard faces that suggested they might draw on you and shoot you down if you so much as spat on your hand. And they weren't cowboys either. They were dressed in black leathers and when they laughed it sounded like rocks churning in a dried-up riverbed.

One of them, the hard-faced man who seemed to be their leader, took a particular interest in Cassidy and the El Jango region.

'El Jango's close by the Chisum spread, ain't it?' he asked.

'Biggest spread in the area,' Cassidy boasted.

'That's what I heard,' the man said. 'Ever hear tell of a man called Flint?' he asked with one eye on Wheeler.

'You mean Tom Flint?' Cassidy said. Now he began to feel a creeping suspicion come over him. Everyone east of the Pecos had heard of Tom Flint and John Chisum.

'Sure, Tom Flint.' The man jeered as though implying he had a long acquaintance with Tom Flint, going back to his childhood. 'Runs the Slashed S outfit. Called himself Man of Blood one time.'

Cassidy said he didn't know about that but had heard Flint was in the Rangers way back.

'OK, Randy,' Rosa piped up. 'Buy the man a drink. He's been riding from El Jango, must be thirsty. He doesn't want to know about Tom Flint.'

That eased the tension somewhat and everybody laughed including Randy, though Randy's laugh was more like a hoot of derision.

Cassidy appreciated the way Rosa had intervened to save him from embarrassment. He was impressed by

Rosa. He liked a woman with courage and Rosa sure had plenty of courage. She was slim and shapely as any woman he had yet met.

The hard-faced man who had expressed an interest in Flint turned out to be Randolph Remarque. Now he drew away and left Cassidy and Rosa alone. Soon the bunch at the bar had started a game of poker.

'Don't mind those galoots,' Rosa murmured quietly to Cassidy. 'They can be wild but they don't mean nothing.' She turned to look at him with her big, rather beautiful eyes. 'What you doing this way, stranger?'

'Just looking,' Cassidy said. He didn't go into details about wanting to go to college and study for the law like his friend Tom Flint junior.

Rosa nodded and smoked. She seemed to understand his reluctance to give chapter and verse. 'You staying somewhere close by?'

Cassidy paused. He didn't want to admit he had thought about sleeping in the open or even possibly in the saloon. He had had a fancy idea that getting away from El Jango and sleeping under the stars might help him to meditate on his uncertain future. The mayor of El Jango had offered him the sheriff's star but he didn't know whether he was ready to take it as a stop-gap measure.

Rosa was still watching him closely. Her dark eyes sort of mesmerized him. 'I know a place close by where you could stay if you had a mind to it,' she said.

That was a crucial moment.

Cassidy hesitated for no more than half a second. Then he nodded. It was to be a turning point in his life.

'So Rosa Ramondo and you became lovers?' Flint suggested.

Cassidy scarcely blinked. Now he had started his story he wouldn't stop until he had spilled it all out.

Yes, he and Rosa became lovers and soon they began to meet in the ruined shack that Baldy had described. Rosa never told Cassidy where she came from or where she went to. She must have had a place to stay close by El Jango. But Cassidy was soon in thrall to her as though she was a wicked witch who had woven a spell of enchantment around him.

Until one day the big cash-in occurred.

'Listen, lover boy,' Rosa whispered one night in the ruined shack. 'I'm going to ask you one big favour.'

'Ask away,' Cassidy said, under her spell.

'You promise to do what I say?' she said.

'You say it and I promise,' he agreed.

Rosa didn't mention the time or the day or which day. She told Cassidy that one time soon he would receive a visit in his office. He should do exactly what the visitor told him to do. Then nobody would get hurt and he would be a rich man – rich enough to go to law school and buy his own law practice one day, maybe quite soon, and then they could be married and settle down where they liked.

Cassidy fell for it, like a catfish snapping at a bait. He didn't mind being locked in his cell for half an hour just so long as nobody got hurt. 'Nobody's going to get hurt,' Rosa soothed. 'You know nothing and everything is going to be all right.'

'I lost my judgement,' Cassidy admitted miserably to Flint. 'That woman put a spell on me and I behaved like a fool.'

Flint didn't contradict him.

'The bank bust might have been OK and I guess I was tempted by the devil in female form,' Cassidy admitted after a moment. 'The terrible thing is that three men got killed. That bank teller and the old feller were just law-abiding citizens doing their duty.' He paused and lowered his gaze. 'And it was my fault Tom junior lost his life.'

There was a moment's silence. Flint shook his head slowly. 'You seen that woman Rosa Ramondo since the hold-up?' He looked directly at Cassidy again. 'Now you tell me the truth about this,' he warned.

Cassidy shook his head in vigorous denial. 'Of course I haven't seen her! And I never will. That woman used me, Flint. She pretended to have love for me but it was just a trick of the devil. Rosa is in with Randolph Remarque right up to her . . .'

'. . . Fancy earrings,' Flint prompted. He thought matters over quietly. 'You seen Remarque again recently?'

'Not since then. I seen him twice, once in the Rio Pecos saloon, Wheeler's place and the second time during the bank bust. That's all. He was the man who came in wearing a red bandanna over his lower face. Though he wore the bandanna, I knew him.'

'You quite sure it was him?'

Cassidy nodded decisively. 'That was Remarque. No

68

doubt. I knew him by his deep ugly voice and I particularly remember his laugh. Like something between a rattlesnake and a death rattle.'

Flint was still considering matters. 'You say that time you saw Remarque he mentioned me?'

Cassidy looked up sharply. 'Yes. He knew you, Mr Flint. He called you Man of Blood in a sneering kind of way and he spoke of the Slashed S.' Cassidy started wringing his hands. 'I know I've done terrible bad things, Mr Flint, and I'm so sorry. What do I do now? I can't face up to the guilt. What do I do, Mr Flint?'

Flint looked at him without flinching. 'You can begin by not punishing yourself. Sure you've done bad and foolish things, Cassidy. And you have to live with that. But you have to keep your head and use it too.'

Cassidy pulled himself up in his seat. 'One thing,' he said, 'I aim to hand in this star as soon as I get back to El Jango.'

Flint shook his head. 'That's what I mean about using your head. That may be the worst thing you can do at the present moment.'

'Why should that be?'

Flint leaned forward and looked Cassidy directly in the eye again. 'You hand in that star people will know what they already suspect, that you helped with the bank bust. They might even take it in mind to put a rope around your neck and string you up somewhere. Jim Stacey in particular was a well-respected member of the community. And so was Tom junior, not to mention the bank teller.'

Cassidy hadn't taken that into account. It occurred

to Flint that he might be a rather defective lawyer if someday he managed to qualify.

'What do you suggest, Mr Flint?' Cassidy asked wretchedly.

'What you do is to hold on to that star and keep quiet about what you said to me. Do your duty in the normal way. Lock up drunks and keep wearing that shooter like you mean business. And keep your ears open. Rosa Ramondo hasn't made contact yet, but that doesn't mean she's given up on you entirely.'

Cassidy's eyes widened. 'You mean she might have other plans?'

Flint grinned. 'We don't know that, do we?'

This had obviously opened up a whole new vista for Cassidy. 'You're asking me to use myself as some kind of bait?' he said.

Flint shrugged. 'I wouldn't put it quite like that,' he said. 'I would say you keep your star and wait. She wants you she'll come back. Then we find out who killed Tom junior and rope the whole lot of them in. It might not work but it could be worth a try.'

That helped to brighten Cassidy up. 'If you think you can trust me,' he said.

It might have been intended as a question but Flint chose to ignore it. 'I heard you're good with a pencil and paper?' he said to Cassidy.

'I can draw if that's what you mean?' Cassidy admitted warily.

'That's what I'm saying,' Flint said. 'I heard you did some drawings of well-known statesmen a little while back. Unless I'm mistaken they printed some of them in the *Las Vegas Gazette.*'

Cassidy considered the question for a while. It was true he had at one time thought he might blossom as an artist; he had the knack of drawing quite amusing pictures of statesmen like Abraham Lincoln and the Governor Lew Wallace.

'What had you in mind, Mr Flint?' he asked.

Flint rose from the table and hunted around for a wad of paper and a stub of pencil he had stashed away on a big sideboard.

'What I want for you to do, Mr Cassidy, is for you to set yourself down right now and draw me two pictures, one of Rosa Ramondo and one of Randolph Remarque. Do you think you can do that?'

Cassidy reached out and took the wad of paper. 'I think I can do that, Mr Flint.'

When Cassidy left the ranch he was a deal easier in his mind and conscience. He had opened up to Flint as though he was visiting a friar at a mission. He felt almost like singing.

But his joy didn't last. As he rode along, his mind went back to Rosa and her protestations of love towards him. At the time he had believed her . . . would have believed her still if it hadn't been for the killing of Stacey and the bank teller, and particularly Tom Flint junior, whose example he had always admired. He and Tom had fished together in a creek close by El Jango, and when he had strained too close to the water to scoop out a fish he had caught and pitched right into the water it was Tom who had reached right down and yanked him out . . . and possibly saved his life.

Cassidy couldn't rub the picture of Tom out of his mind. Neither could he cast aside the image of Rosa with her big beautiful eyes and her open, appealing expression. She still seemed to hover like a loving Cheshire cat as he started down Spiky Gully, heading back towards El Jango, and he couldn't believe she had betrayed him for the sake of gold and revenge.

Suddenly he heard a horse riding up on him from behind, at first quite distant and then much closer. Could be Jason Flint, he thought. Maybe he wants to pin me down with another question. Just like Jason to leap into the saddle straight off and follow me before I get back to El Jango, he thought. That was Jason's impetuous nature.

But this rider wasn't Jason Flint. It was another hard-case he couldn't recall having seen before, a man who sat in the saddle with the ease of someone who was used to hard riding.

'Hi there, stranger!' the man called out. 'Mind if I ride along with you a piece!'

This was unusual – a little too obviously polite and suspicious.

'You headed for El Jango?' Cassidy asked the stranger.

The man gave a wry, rather crooked grin and showed a mouth of broken nicotine-stained teeth. 'Could be, and then again, maybe not. I see you're wearing a star on your vest. I guess you might be Sheriff Cassidy.'

'I'm Cassidy,' Cassidy agreed. 'I been Cassidy since I was born.'

The man laughed somewhat discordantly. 'I'm Fielder. You won't have heard of me.' He wrinkled his nose in speculation. 'By my calculation, you're riding in from the Slashed S ranch. Could that be right?'

Cassidy felt more uneasy now. He glanced sideways at the man and saw he carried a Colt revolver, cross-draw, high on his hip where he could reach it easily as he rode. In fact he was stroking the butt of the gun with his fingers as though he had particular affection for it.

'I had business with Mr Flint,' Cassidy said.

An ugly grin slanted across Fielder's face. 'Business with Tom Flint, eh?' he jeered.

Cassidy turned towards him in the saddle. He had a bad feeling now . . . a feeling he might regret this unexpected interview. 'We do talk from time to time,' he admitted. 'What's that to you, stranger?'

'Don't you think it might be unhealthy to mix with Tom Flint?' Fielder said with quiet menace. 'After all, Flint is a dead man walking. Living men don't talk to the dead. You know Randy Remarque would be none too pleased about that, especially after what you promised him.'

Cassidy was now bristling all over with alertness and fear. 'I promised Remarque nothing,' he objected.

'Randy doesn't think that way. He figures it different. He thinks you're one of the bunch, and the bunch needs loyalty. You took the cut and you're one of the bunch.'

Cassidy riled up. 'I took no cut so far. I just agreed to the conditions as long as there was no killing.'

'Randy doesn't see that. Neither does Rosa. They feel

a big sense of grievance. So they asked me to ride down and talk to you about it.'

This was the first Cassidy had heard of Rosa since before the robbery. The memory of her large, appealing eyes returned suddenly. What could this disgusting critter have to do with her? He felt the hot blood rushing to his face.

'Rosa wants to talk to me, she'll talk to me herself,' he retorted. He eased his right foot out of his stirrup ready to kick out at the man and spur away. Or should he slide out of his saddle and dive for cover? Or maybe keep talking, playing for time?

Fielder was laughing. 'Rosa don't want to talk to you. She figures you're nothing more than a rat crawling in a ditch. That's what Rosa thinks.'

'Who the hell are you, anyway?' Cassidy roared in his face.

Fielder was still shaking with laughter. 'Like I said, the name's Fielder. You ain't seen me before. I wasn't in on the bank bust in El Jango. That's because I had other fish to fry. But I was there in spirit, sure enough. I'm a Regulator like the rest of the boys. And your friend Flint, or Man of Blood as he calls himself, is in line to be regulated.'

The word *regulated* seemed to echo down the pass like a mocking laugh.

Cassidy saw that Fielder's hand had stopped stroking the butt of his Colt. This was getting uglier and clearer. He tensed himself, ready to spring. He couldn't wait any longer for developments. He struck out at Fielder's horse and kicked it right in the belly close by the man's knee. The horse whinnied and lurched away. Fielder slid sideways and jerked on the reins to right himself. This could be Cassidy's chance to get himself clear. He swung his own horse to butt against the other horse so he could push Fielder right out of the saddle and get the drop on him before anything worse happened.

But Fielder was an old and experienced killer As he slid aside he managed to steady himself by clutching at the saddle horn with his left hand. At the same moment, he drew his Colt clear of its holster and fired two shots into Cassidy's body at point-blank range. *Bam! Bam!*

The sound of the shots echoed right down the gully!

The bullets struck Cassidy just below the ribcage. They jerked him right out of his saddle. His horse reared, throwing him into the air and on to the ground where he sprawled, gasping and clutching at his ribs. Then he struggled to reach for his gun . . . but it was too late.

Fielder steadied his horse and dismounted. He was a short, bow-legged man. He left the horses and ambled round to Cassidy's writhing body.

'Thought you'd get the drop on me, did you, little man?' he sneered.

He bent low and looked into Cassidy's dying eyes. He grinned again in the same ugly fashion.

'By the way, I forgot to mention something. Rosa asked me to give you a sweet and loving message specially from her to you. Goodbye, sweetheart. Sleep well.'

He drew his Colt, cocked it, and fired two shots into

Cassidy's head. Cassidy jerked and kicked out with one leg. Then he rolled over and lay still. He hadn't even got to firing his Smith & Wesson .38.

Fielder looked at the barrel of his Colt .44 thoughtfully. Then he holstered it.

'Sleep tight and well, little man,' he muttered.

He caught his horse, mounted up with leisure, and rode on down the gully.

CHAPTER SIX

The pictures that Cassidy had drawn of Rosa Ramondo and Randolph Remarque were surprisingly clear and professional.

'What made you think about it?' Marie marvelled when she saw them spread on the kitchen table.

'Saw what he did in the *Las Vegas Gazette*,' Flint said. 'He should have drawn for a living. And that *hombre's* face reminds me of something from the past; I can't figure what.'

Even Jason pored over the portraits with amazing interest. He appeared to have calmed down considerably after Cassidy's visit. The faces in the portraits seemed to stare back at him with surprising fierceness and intensity. The man Randolph Remarque had high cheekbones and drooping eyelids as though he was looking at the world with calculation and hatred. That was the face that nudged at Flint's memory.

Rosa Ramondo was altogether different. Her eyes were bright and focused, staring out with an erotic challenge. Yet there was something similar about the two

77

faces that he couldn't figure. One thing came across quite clearly: Cassidy was still holding more than a burning torch for Rosa.

'My, that's an attractive female,' Jason breathed.

'These are the people who killed your brother!' Marie reminded him.

'Thought I could use these,' Flint said. 'You look at them long enough they get fixed in your memory. Then, when the time comes, you know exactly who you have to deal with.'

'But when will the time come? And what do we do to make it happen?' Jason asked.

Flint reeled in the two portraits and stowed them away in the drawer in the sideboard. He was still figuring which way to jump.

'The Rio Pecos saloon might be the answer to that,' he muttered.

Come morning, Jason didn't take breakfast with the family. During the early hours he had lit out without a word to anyone. During the night he had slipped the portraits out of the drawer and ridden off with them tucked under his vest.

'That boy's gone!' Marie cried out in alarm. 'He rode out just before sun-up. I heard him! I thought it was one of the crew!'

Flint had heard him too but had been too sleepy to put two and two together. Then he saw the note Marie was holding up for him. It was in Jason's scratchy hand-writing, and it read simply:

Sorry I couldn't stay. I know there's a lot to do around the place, but someone has to move on those killers and I guess it has to be me. You don't seem ready to do anything and someone has to. So I'm going after those goddamn killers and, when I find them, I mean to blast them to hell for my brother Tom. Hope to see you later when all this is over. If not, look after yourselves.

Sorry again, but that's the way it is.

Jason.

Marie was gasping with amazement and horror. 'What are we going to do? Those ornery gunmen have killed one of my sons and now they will take my other boy!'

Flint said nothing. His rugged features had become the colour of ash. 'Did Jason take anything with him?' he asked grimly.

Marie was checking the larder. 'Other than his guns, he took supplies,' she said. 'That boy means business. He'll be far off by now.'

Flint was dragging on his range clothes: tying his bandanna against the dust; putting on his leather vest; buckling up his chaps and spurs. Then he checked his Colt and Old Reliable.

'You're going after him,' Marie said. Although she knew it was inevitable, she was afraid: could be she would lose both a son and a husband. She was thinking: this man, who is my husband, is too old for this. But Flint was as tough as rawhide. He had endured much hardship, as when the gunman Wolf had tried to shoot him and again when that bull of a man Big Blue had tried to kill Marie and him both. And that had brought them together, and she prayed this wouldn't separate them again!

'I want to come with you,' she said. 'I can shoot too. You owe me that. These are my sons!'

Flint paused, as though he was considering the matter. Then he took her by the shoulders. 'You know I can't let you do that,' he said. 'You've got to keep the place together. The boys out there on the ranch need guidance and control. Without me and Jason, you're the only one can do it.'

Marie had to agree. 'Promise me you'll come back in one piece?' she said.

Flint smoothed back her hair and hugged her close. 'Don't you worry,' he said. 'I aim to come back and bring Jason with me.'

Back in El Jango around midmorning Baldy Barlow was mooching about in his usual way, poking his nose into Frenchy's diner in the hope of getting a snack and looking in on Madame Renoir in her emporium. Though he greeted everyone cheerfully enough, he knew in the marrow of his bones that something was wrong. Baldy lacked a great deal but he had certain faculties that other men would have mocked and dismissed as absurd. Now he had a strange but not unfamiliar feeling in his head. Could he be about to have another fit? But, no, this feeling was different, like a storm gathering on the horizon yet reluctant to break.

He was in the middle of the main drag trying to make up his mind which way to go, when he saw the horse and recognized it at once. It was all lathered up from galloping and it came to Baldy and tossed its head. Baldy reached up, took the reins and muttered soothing words to the beast. Then he saw what he was already dreading: there was blood dripping from the horse's mane and more blood on the saddle.

Joe Slocum, the mayor, had just left Frenchy's after a brief doughnut snack and a coffee when he saw Baldy leading the horse across the street and hitching it to the rail. He noticed that the horse was kind of spooky and frothing at the mouth.

'What you doing with the sheriff's horse, Baldy?' he asked suspiciously.

Badly looked up at him in alarm. 'Sheriff Cassidy's been shot!' he said.

'What the hell you talking about?' Slocum blustered. 'Cassidy will be in his office. Always is at this hour of the day, 'less he has pressing business.'

Instead of bowing his head as usual and backing off, Badly stamped his foot and looked aggressive. 'I say the sheriff's been shot!' he insisted. 'I know it for sure.'

Slocum cussed and moved forward to reprove the halfwit. Then he saw the blood on Baldy's hand and more staining the saddle. 'Where d'you find this horse?' he demanded.

'He just came in down the trail. I tell you Sheriff Cassidy's been shot down. He's lying out there some-where in Spiky Gully.'

'How do you know that, you damned fool?' the mayor roared.

Baldy stood his ground. 'I know it, Mr Slocum,

81

because I seed it in my head.'

Slocum looked at him with alarm and disgust. He knew Baldy claimed to see a lot of things in his head since he was half-crazed. But on this occasion, the mayor faltered. 'You mean you can see Cassidy lying there wounded? How come?'

Baldy shook his head. 'I seen him, Mr Slocum. And he ain't wounded. I think he's dead.' His face was contorted as though he was about to have a fit, but his eyes were staring bright, and his face was the colour of mouldy cheese.

'Dead!' Slocum echoed. He began to take Baldy more seriously. 'Wait here!' he said. 'Wait while I see what to do.'

The mayor blustered away looking for help and support. He would get a few men together and ride out to Spiky Gully to check on Baldy's unlikely vision.

Jason rode towards the Pecos in the early hours of dawn. He knew exactly where he was headed: the Rio Pecos saloon. He also knew that Cassidy had been there once, maybe more than once. Jason knew he was riding full tilt into danger, but he didn't give a damn. Just as long as he could catch up with his brother's killers and put them under the sod.

He had taken a good hard look at Cassidy's pencil portraits before he tucked them away under his vest and they were imprinted on his brain and soul so that he would know those killers anywhere. He even conjured them in the air like phantoms as he rode along.

The sun came up over his shoulder like it meant to encourage him and urge him on, and this gave him a kind of superstitious hope.

When in late morning he reached the Rio Pecos saloon he saw a good bunch of horses tethered at the rail and knew he had hit the right place. The Rio Pecos saloon was no more than an inn for anyone who might be passing by. The owner, he figured, must keep himself and his wife alive by running a small spread with hens and maybe a pig or two.

Jason tied his horse to the rail and went in under the *ramada*. He paused at the swing doors and loosened his Colt in its holster. Then he pushed back the doors, went right into the saloon and saw the mountainous figure of Wheeler standing behind the bar. Wheeler looked straight over at him and the grin congealed on his lips. Even a big talker like Wheeler could read the expression on the face of a man who was about to stir up big trouble.

But Jason Flint wasn't interested in Wheeler. His attention switched to the figures crouched over the bar slightly to the left. He saw they had been pitching into ham and eggs, but they stopped as one man and turned to stare at the newcomer.

The man Jason recognized immediately from the picture as Randolph Remarque had his hand on the butt of his Colt halfway to drawing, as if he already expected trouble. Clearly he was no slouch with a gun.

Jason was still young. He knew about ranching but, at that time, little about tactics or finesse in personal dealings. As a youth he had practised shooting at bottles and cans in the yard, but, though he was brave to fool-hardy, he was no shootist. So he stood by the swing doors and said: 'I'm looking for a man called Remarque.' His voice came out startlingly loud.

Wheeler stooped and reached for a shooter he had tucked under the bar in case of emergencies. Randolph Remarque swung to face Jason on the stool with his hand still on the butt of his gun. 'You looking for Randolph Remarque?' he said. 'You found him, saddle slide.'

There was a rumble of laughter from the other men at the bar.

Jason stepped forward a pace and saw the other hardcases were already halfway to drawing on him. Remarque first, he thought. I kill him, then worry about the others. He knew he couldn't take them all out but he suddenly didn't give a damn about that!

'You got some grievance with me, trail bum?' Remarque asked playfully. He had half-closed calculating eyes like in the portrait, but the grin on his lips betrayed a desire to play cat-and-mouse with what he saw as a greenhorn wrangler.

'That's what I aim to find out,' Jason said.

Remarque half-turned to sneer at his *compadres*. 'How d'you reckon to do that, buddy boy?' He laughed. His laughter was deep but jagged like rocks rolling in a dry gully.

Jason breathed in slowly. 'If you're Remarque, you killed my brother Tom Flint junior and robbed the bank in El Jango. And that's enough for me.'

Something lit up in Remarque's eyes when heard the

name Flint. He slid from the bar stool, stood up straight and nodded his head. He was a little over average height and was as lean as a coyote.

'So you're the kid brother?' he said. 'And Tom Flint, the Man of Blood must be your daddy. Is that right, boy?' The word boy rang out with derision and the men at the bar, including the bartender Wheeler, started rocking with laughter as though Remarque had made a clever joke at Jason's expense.

Jason turned pink as a cooked lobster but he didn't laugh. 'You care to step outside, Remarque, and we can settle this matter man to man.'

That made the slit-eyed man laugh even more. 'Man to man!' he sneered. 'What in hell's name do you know about man to man? You still got wet behind your baby ears.'

Jason felt a surge of adrenaline in his veins, and, before he could think of what to say next, he had his six-shooter cocked and half-drawn.

Remarque was ahead of him. His own shooter came out like a flash in a winter sky. Wheeler ducked behind the bar, struggling to get a grip on his emergency gun. Remarque's *compadres* were leaning forward, halfway to drawing. Seven red-hot bullets were about to thud into Jason's foolhardy body! But nobody fired a shot!

'Now, boys, what are you thinking of? We don't want shooting in here! Mr Wheeler hates violence. So put up your guns and keep the peace!'

Everybody froze as if some fairy from an ancient tale had waved her wand.

Jason heard the voice which was mellow and soft. It

85

came from his right, and he saw from the corner of his eye the woman in Cassidy's pencil drawing. Cassidy was a good artist but he couldn't do justice to what Jason saw. She was some beautiful woman but it was the eyes that even Cassidy's drawing couldn't do justice to. If Jason had been familiar with the work of William Shakespeare he might have thought of Juliet on the balcony at that instant.

Then the picture unfroze. The boys at the bar seemed to melt a little. Even Remarque started grinning, as if the world was all a big joke.

'Whatever you say, Rosa,' he drawled.

'OK,' one of the others agreed. 'That's right, whatever you say, Rosa.'

The men at the bar and Randolph Remarque slid their shooters back into their holsters and returned to their ham and eggs.

'Now, Mr Flint, why don't you put that shooter back and let it rest,' Rosa said.

Jason uncocked his pistol and let it rest in its holster.

Rosa Ramondo slid right up to Jason and fixed her hypnotic eyes on him. 'So you must be Jason Flint, Tom Flint's son,' she murmured. 'Why don't you sit right down and get your breath back, have a drink and a bite of chow. You might be kinda hungry after that long ride.' She turned to Wheeler, who was fighting to get his breath back behind the bar. 'Bring the man a slice of that good ham and some eggs as well. We have things to discuss here.'

'Whatever you say, Rosa,' the big man whined.

*

It was rash to promise to Marie to bring us both back alive, Tom Flint thought as he rode steadily on the trail towards the Pecos and then took a south in the direction of Fort Sumner. The Rio Pecos saloon was some three miles short of Fort Sumner. He knew that was where Jason would be headed, straight into the dragon's den.

Flint admired his younger son's grit but hated his rash way of sticking his head into the hot oven. Though Flint had never been to the Rio Pecos saloon, he had heard about it and knew the owner was a braggart called Wheeler.

He drew close to the saloon in the early afternoon. He eased Old Reliable in its sheath and made sure his Peacemaker rode in its holster nice and smooth. The place seemed dead in the heat of the day. There was no sound but for the drone of insects and the faint hum of wind in the chaparral.

Not a soul about. The place seemed creepy and half-asleep in the heat-shimmer of the day. He dismounted and led his horse into the shade where it could take its ease and drink. A small Mexican boy appeared out of the shadows, took charge of the horse and promised he would see it was fed.

Flint pushed open the swing doors and took a look inside. Still as a sleeping dog. It was several seconds before he could focus on the man in the wicker chair sleeping with a newspaper spread over his belly.

Flint walked over to the bar and laid his Peacemaker across it, none too quietly. Steve Wheeler stirred behind the paper. His eyes shot open in alarm, and he struggled to his feet.

'Didn't hear you come in!' he said breathlessly. 'You must have a quiet tread like an Apache Indian.' He giggled as though he had made a fine joke.

Flint looked him over and saw that Cassidy had given a pretty good description: huge belly flowing over the buckle of his jeans, black moustache like a bat drooping over his chops, eyes that darted every which way as though they didn't know where to fix.

'You must be Steve Wheeler,' Flint said.

'Sure, I'm Wheeler. Pleased to meet you, Mr . . .' He extended a large rather smooth hand across the bar. 'Should I know you?'

Flint didn't take the offered hand. He preferred to look into a man's eyes and read him. Steve Wheeler had eyes that didn't look at you properly. They seemed to dart about, uncertain where to rest. Flint saw that in their darting they kept glancing nervously at the Peacemaker lying across the bar.

'Can I get you a drink?' Wheeler said. 'It sure is a thirsty day.'

Flint nodded. 'I'll take a beer.'

Wheeler poured the beer until it foamed up over the rim of the glass. Flint saw that his hand was shaking slightly.

'You come from far?' Wheeler enquired cheerfully.

Flint took the beer and sipped it. To do the barman credit the drink was cool and refreshing.

'I'm looking for a young man,' Flint said. 'Must have passed through an hour or two back. I wonder, did you happen to see him?'

Wheeler fumbled with his moustaches with nervous

fingers. 'Can't say I remember. What was this young *hombre* like?' The eyes were still darting to and fro like pool balls trying to find a pocket.

Flint gave Jason's description. Early twenties; hair inclined to be sandy; wiry and fit-looking; around five eleven to six feet tall.

'Oh, yes. Now I do remember, there was a young guy in earlier,' Wheeler said. 'Could be the man you're looking for. Are you a United States marshal looking for someone on the run by any chance?'

'Not exactly,' Flint said. 'This young man happens to be my son.'

Wheeler grinned wide like the Cheshire Cat sitting in the tree. 'Sure!' he said. 'Now I believe I can see the likeness! I think I seed you before some place. Heard about you too. You must be Tom Flint, the famous Indian fighter!'

He reached across the counter and offered Flint his hand again. This time Flint touched the hand briefly. It reminded him of a fish he once caught in the Rio Grande.

'I done a bit of Indian fighting myself,' Wheeler said, his eyes gleaming with self-importance. 'Fought with Kit Carson against the Navajo. That was some fight, I can tell you.' He started into a detailed description of how he scalped a warrior he'd managed to overpower. 'Strange thing is, for all that the man survived. Head like a bullet, eh?' Wheeler went into a fit of wheezing laughter. 'Did you ever scalp one of them there Comanches?' he asked.

'Come to think of it, I never did,' Flint said wryly. He

leaned forward across the bar. 'So you do remember seeing my son?' He was tapping against the butt of the Peacemaker with his index finger. 'Like I said, I'm talking about maybe two or three hours back.'

'Sure! Sure!' Wheeler chortled nervously. 'Like I said. Good-looking boy. Dropped by several hours back like you just mentioned. Took a bite of breakfast here before he rode on.'

Flint nodded grimly. Now he was getting somewhere. 'Here's another question for you. You happen to know a man called Remarque – Randolph Remarque, and a woman called Rosa Ramondo?'

Wheeler had stopped chortling. His jaw dropped as though he was about to take a bite of deer meat. Then he got a hold on himself. He rubbed the side of his cheek with his pudgy hand. 'People come and go here, Mr Flint,' he said thoughtfully. 'I don't ask for names or references, and generally don't get none. I aim to stay out of things and get on with my job here. I run a little farm with hens and pigs out there. Me and my wife mean to settle to a peaceable life and mind our own business here.'

Flint nodded slowly. 'They tell met Rosa Ramondo is a particularly good-looking woman,' he said.

Wheeler's eyebrows shot up suddenly. 'Oh, she's a good-looking woman all right!' Then he checked himself and put on his thoughtful mode again. 'I mean, we get a lot of good-looking women in here. You'd be surprised. Not to say we encourage the bad type of woman, you know.'

Flint was still tapping insistently on the butt of the

Peacemaker. 'So you do know who they are, Remarque and Rosa Ramondo?'

Wheeler put on a beam of a smile and shock his head. 'Oh, no, I never seen those folks before, not to my knowing. I could have done and then I might not. I don't ask too many questions around here. That's the truth and that's what I told your son before he rode on.'

Flint fixed his eyes on the bar owner. 'You happen to see which way he rode?'

Wheeler reflected for a moment. 'Sure, yes, I do remember now. That young man took a bite of food and then he rode off in the direction of Sunnyside. That's some eight miles north of here. I think that's where he said he was headed.'

'You sure about that?' Flint asked Wheeler.

'Oh, I'm sure . . . I'm sure,' Wheeler assured him. 'That's where the man said he was headed.'

Flint gave him a hard stare and slid his Peacemaker off the bar.

As he stepped out of the Rio Pecos saloon he knew he had a deal of thinking to do. Wheeler was a none-too-accomplished liar and a big bag of horse shit. And Flint didn't aim to waste his time listening to any more fables about how many Indians he had killed.

As Flint went to find his horse, a small figure appeared out of the shadows to beckon to him. 'Señor Flint,' the boy hissed, 'I feed your horse very good. Like all your horses it is very good horse. You look after them good.'

Flint bent towards the Mexican boy. 'How did you know my name?' he asked.

91

The boy came out into the light. 'I know you, *señor*. You save my life.'

'How come?' But before the boy spoke again, Flint recognized him. It was the boy he had stopped them from hanging when they caught him and his father stealing two of his steers.

'That was a good thing you did for me,' the boy said. 'Those men had the rope around my neck and I was up on the horse's back. It was what you gringos call a close calling.'

Flint took the horse by the reins and looked down at the boy, who could have been twelve, maybe fifteen according to how well he had been fed. He had a clear picture of that moment when the boy and his father had been about to swing from that skeleton-like tree, how the boy's father had blubbered and prayed and pleaded for the boy's life, and how the boy had been brave; though, when they took him down from the horse, he had thrown up beside the tree.

'You were a brave kid,' Flint told him.

'Thank you, *señor*,' the boy said proudly. Flint saw he looked a lot brighter here in the stable. His expression was almost mischievous and intelligent.

The boy put his finger to his lips and peered back into the gloom of the stable. 'I tell you something, *señor*,' he whispered. 'I tell you something about your son.'

Flint suddenly started listening intently. 'What do you want to tell me, *compadre*?'

The boy sidled in closer. 'You save me, *señor*, I help to save your son. Your son was to kill me on the tree but

92

you saved me and my father. So I tell you what happen to your son right here.' The boy glanced back nervously at Rio Peos saloon.

Flint paused for a moment, looking down at the boy, who switched to stare eagerly up at him. It crossed his mind that the boy was a plant, put there to tell him more lies. Wheeler was such an ornery liar he might get up to any misleading trick. 'What's in this for you?' he asked the boy.

The boy drew back slightly as if he was afraid he might be beaten. 'I tell you, there's nothing in this for me,' he hissed. 'This man Wheeler, he is very bad man. He kick me. I show you bruises. You help me get away from here, I tell you everything, where they took your son . . . everything . . .'

Where they took your son: the words rang ominously in Flint's mind. So Jason was taken somewhere. Did he go willingly? Was there some kind of struggle? And why should those killers want to take him anyway?

'You got a horse?' Flint asked the boy.

'I got my burro,' the boy said eagerly.

'Get your burro,' Flint said. 'We ride away from here and you tell me everything.'

'Sí, señor,' the boy said keenly.

Marie was about her usual chores when the riders came over the hill. She grabbed a Winchester and stood by the door. She recognized Mayor Slocum and several other men and, to her surprise, Baldy Barlow. Baldy was slightly behind the mayor and he rode surprisingly well considering everyone thought he was no good for anything.

The mayor raised his hand and the whole posse drew up close to the ranch house. Marie saw at once that something was wrong and her thoughts sprang immediately to her husband and her son.

'What happened?' she called out in alarm.

'Someone is killed,' one of the posse replied in a high voice.

The mayor made a move to dismount but, despite his disability, Baldly was ahead of him. He hobbled towards Marie. 'It's Sheriff Cassidy,' he said. 'He's been killed in Spiky Gully!'

'Shot four times,' Slocum confirmed. 'Twice through the chest and twice through the head. Coward must have pumped two in his head as he lay on the ground.' Slocum wasn't going to let a halfwit outdo him when it came to gruesome details.

Marie stared at them with disbelief. Cassidy might have been weak and none too wise, but he had tried to make up for his wrongs and come clean with the truth. She had thought the posse had come to bring bad news about her husband Tom or Jason, her son. So Slocum's words came as a bitter relief.

'You'd better all come into the house,' she said.

CHAPTER SEVEN

The kid's name was Juan – Juan Darringo. It turned out he was a small fifteen. He lived with his mother and father and his two sisters and the toothless grandfather who had stepped in to save them under the tree that looked like a blackened skeleton. The reason Juan was so small was that his family lived very close to the bone and sometimes they had nothing to eat. But Juan was intelligent and enterprising. He had ambition and intended to do well for himself. That was how he had got the job looking after horses in Wheeler's saloon, though Wheeler treated him like a slave.

Wheeler paid very little for Juan's services. So the kid had already decided to leave when the episode with Jason Flint occurred. When Juan wasn't tending the horses he hung around picking up useful bits of information. When you're poor, you learn to listen and get wise or starve. You never knew what you could learn by just listening and watching, and, because he was small, Juan had the ability to hang about in the shadows and behind half-open doors. That's how he happened to be

there when Jason came into the Rio Pecos saloon looking for Randolph Remarque and Rosa Ramondo. Juan
saw the whole thing and he recognized Jason immediately from when he had almost swung from that dead
tree.

It had happened like this.

Rosa Ramondo was a beautiful young woman who
had the art of bewitching a man, mostly with her eyes.
Juan had known her since she was a girl. Half Mexican
and half Anglo, he said. Came from back East, around
Arkansas somewhere, he thought.

When Rosa intervened to stop the shoot-out, Juan was
surprised. He ducked his head down behind the door
and waited. But there was no shooting. Everything went
dead quiet, as if a ghost or something had entered the
room. There was no eating, either. Wheeler never got to
bringing that big breakfast Rosa had ordered for Jason.
Instead there was a degree of whispering and then a
muffled bumping sound. Juan popped his head around
the door and saw Jason staggering back and sprawling
unconscious on the floor. One of Remarque's sidekicks,
a bow-legged *hombre* called Fielder, had snuck up behind
Jason and pistol-whipped him real hard. Fielder had just
ridden in and had come into the saloon real quiet and
got a signal from Remarque's eyes.

'Want me to shoot him dead?' Fielder had asked
Remarque as Jason lay helpless and bloody on the
saloon floor.

'Leave him,' Remarque said. 'I have other plans.'

'That was a real hard blow to the back of his head!'
Juan said to Flint. 'Fit to bust a man's skull!'

'My God, I think you killed him!' Rosa had said. 'Why did you hit him so hard? We don't want him dead. We want him alive. That way we get Tom Flint!'

Rosa got down on her knees and looked at Jason's injuries. Jason was bleeding real bad from the wound on the back of his head. Though he could have been mistaken for dead, he was still breathing.

'You did the right thing,' Remarque said to Fielder. 'I might have had to shoot him. Fact is, I nearly did. This young fool is worth more to us alive than dead. Like Rosa said, that way we stand to get Tom Flint.'

'Like you nearly got him in Spiky Gully, you mean?' Rosa mocked.

That nettled Remarque. 'Could have got him there,' he boasted. 'That was just to remind him we're on his trail. Anyway, I got the horse, didn't I?'

'You got the horse! That sure is a big deal!' Rosa laughed.

Someone in the bunch gave a nervous cackle.

'Sure I got the horse,' Remarque said. 'Gave Flint something to smoke his pipe on. Crawled away quick like a lizard. I wasn't going to fall for that one!'

'Don't know why you're so dead set on Flint,' Rosa said. 'He's only another man got stuck in your craw. Time we concentrated on other things.'

'Flint killed my pa,' Remarque reminded her. 'Killed your pa too, remember. This is a matter of honour.'

The boys laughed as though the word *honour* was bad medicine to them.

They rolled Jason over and found the two pencil portraits in the inside pocket of his vest. 'What's this?'

Remarque said. 'Looks like the kid's been taking drawing lessons.'

Juan saw Rosa spread the drawings out on the floor. 'These are drawings of me and you,' she said in astonishment. 'This Flint boy has been carrying our pictures around with him.'

Remarque took the portraits and carried them over to the bar. Juan couldn't see that part of the bar properly, but he judged the whole bunch of them were crowding over the drawings.

'That's purty good picture-making,' the voice of Fielder said. 'Looks awful much like you too, Randy.'

'You know who did these?' Rosa said. 'That's not this Flint boy. That's Cassidy's work. I've seen it before in the *Gazette*.'

'I've seen some too,' Remarque marvelled. 'One of the governor and some other high-toned guy I can't remember.'

'What does this mean, Randy?' one of the other sidekicks said in surprise.

'What it means is Cassidy can't keep his mouth shut. He's too belly-scared to do anything himself. So he draws pictures for the Flints. So they can do the shit,' Remarque growled.

'Didn't I tell you we should never had trusted that bastard?' Fielder said. 'Anyway, you don't need to worry no more about Cassidy. I took him out in Spiky Gully this morning, like you said, Randy.'

That announcement came as a shock, especially to Rosa. Juan peeped round the door as she straightened her back and stared at Remarque. 'You didn't have to kill Cassidy,' she said. 'That was my deal. I could have handled Cassidy.'

'Sure,' Remarque sneered. 'You took a shine to that tin star man. I warned you about that. Anyway, Cassidy knew the deal. So he can't complain.'

'Can't now anyways,' Fielder laughed.

'Cassidy didn't know the deal!' Rosa retorted. 'And it wasn't part of the deal to get trigger-happy and shoot down the bank teller and that old man with the Winchester.'

'And we didn't have to pile in on the Santa Fe stage like that, either?' another voice piped in.

'Gave us the chance to kill another Flint for you, Randy,' a deeper voice interjected.

There was a momentary pause for reflection. 'What's done is done,' Remarque said. 'Good thing about Cassidy. You never trusted him anyway.'

Now Rosa spoke up again. 'That killing was unnecessary. You know that, Fielder, and I know that. It should never have happened.'

'You want egg food,' Remarque said, 'you got to break a few eggs. What's done is done. We might have to break a few more when we do the Las Vegas job.'

'Just so long as you get this boy out of here so I can mop up the floor,' Wheeler said. 'After that you can do what you damned well like with him. It makes no never mind to me.'

'Don't you worry none about that, Wheeler,' Remarque sneered. 'You just keep your big blabbery mouth shut and everything's going to be all right. You hear me?'

'I hear you good,' Wheeler said. He spoke in a high whinney cur's voice, as if Remarque gave him the skitters.

They rolled Jason over and tied him up like a bleeding pig.

'What do we do now?' one of Remarque's sidekicks asked.

'What d'you think we do?' Remarque said contemptuously. 'We pull out of here and we take this young fool Flint with us. When he comes to, he won't know what hit him. Could have been a railroad locomotive!'

They started hauling Jason up on to his feet though it was obvious he couldn't walk; he was still unconscious.

'Wait a minute!' Rosa said. 'I think we should bind up the guy. We don't want him to die on us, do we?'

'Good thinking,' Remarque said. 'He dies on us, we lose Tom Flint. We don't want that.'

So Wheeler disappeared into the back of the saloon and brought bandages and they bound Jason up so he looked like a snowman from the neck upward.

Then they carried him outside, laid him across a horse's back and rode off in a bunch. But not before Remarque had leaned across the bar and grabbed Wheeler by the collar and pulled him close so he looked like a big fish just pulled out of the sea.

'Listen, you big pile of shit,' Remarque said. 'Remember, you're in this with the rest of us. You get your cut like everyone else. So keep your mouth shut, you hear me?'

'I know that, Mr Remarque,' Wheeler gasped out.

'And I appreciate it too.'

When the whole bunch had left, Wheeler fell back behind the bar and started to sob like a baby.

Some Indian fighter!

'You know where they were headed?' Flint asked the boy.

For some minutes he had been unable to speak. Juan's description of the pistol-whipping and Jason sprawling on the floor of the bar with blood gushing from the back of his head made him sick with fear for Jason's life. Tom junior was dead and now Jason might be about to follow. It was bad enough for him, but, when he thought how Marie might take it, his flesh bristled with horror and fury.

Young Juan considered the question. 'They got a cabin somewhere down in the Bosque Redondo,' he said. 'I hear them talking about it one time.'

'So what Wheeler said about going in the Sunnyside direction was all hogwash,' Flint surmised.

They were riding together, the boy on his burro and Flint on his high mount.

What Juan said about the Bosque Redondo made sense. After the Navajo had been defeated and expelled from the Canyon de Chelly they were forced to settle with the Mescalero Apache in the Bosque Redondo, which was probably the most barren part of New Mexico from their point of view. After five years of near starvation they had been allowed to return to the Canyon de Chelly. So everyone now avoided the Bosque Redondo, which was a good place for thieves and

101

desperadoes to hang out.

As well as thinking about Jason and what his fate might have been, Flint strayed back into what Juan had recounted so vividly about what had been said in the Rio Pecos saloon. *He killed my pa and he killed your pa, too.* The light began to dawn. Randolph Remarque and Rosa Ramondo were kids of a man Flint had killed and now they thirsted for revenge. According to Juan it was Remarque who had gunned down on him in Spiky Gully, but Remarque had not intended to kill him – just to warn him and scare him.

And another thing was becoming clearer: these mad killers had not only robbed the bank in El Jango, shooting two innocent men and then going on to rob the Santa Fe stage and killing his son Tom Flint junior; they were now intent on carrying out another robbery in Las Vegas.

Flint suddenly reined in and looked down at the Mexican boy. 'Listen, compadre,' he said, 'you done a good thing telling me what happened in the Rio Pecos. Now you ride back to your family. When this mess is over you come to the ranch. I aim to make life good for you and your family. You have my word on that.'

'*Sí, señor*!' the boy said brightly.

Flint leaned down from the saddle and took the boy's hand. '*Adios, amigo.*'

'*Adios*, Señor Flint. May God go with you.'

That would be a good deal, Flint thought.

The boy shook down on Flint's hand. Then he turned and Flint watched him ride away east on his burro.

*

Flint didn't ride on to the Bosquo Redondo. Instead he turned his horse and rode back to the Rio Pecos saloon. Still there were no horses by the tethering rail and everything seemed quiet as a bone yard. But it was ink-black under the *ramada* and he could feel the eyes watching him.

No more kid gloves, he thought as he drew rein and surveyed the building. Then there was a flash and wild shot from the shadows and a Winchester bullet whined, not close, but close enough.

'Keep away, Flint!' Wheeler's voice sang out. 'I don't want no more trouble here!'

Flint unsheathed Old Reliable and held her high. 'Stop fooling around, Wheeler,' he said. 'A man could get himself killed taking wild shots like that.'

'You think I can't shoot straight?' Wheeler sang out again. Though his voice sounded more resolute than when he was telling stories in the saloon, it still had an edgy whine about it.

Flint brought Old Reliable down, trained her on the shadows where the flash had come from. 'Like you shot those Navajo braves,' he said.

He shifted Old Reliable and fired a shot into the shadows under the ramada. There was a scuffling sound.

'You nearly killed me there,' Wheeler complained.

'Next round I will kill you,' Flint promised, 'just like the rat you are.'

The door of the saloon was thrust open and a large

woman showed. She was almost as big in the girth as Wheeler and she toted a shotgun. 'What in tarnation's going on out here?' she cried.

'Man tried to kill me,' Wheeler complained.

The woman came out on to the porch and steadied the shotgun so she could get a good shot at Flint. Flint figured she might be better with a gun than her husband.

'If I might suggest it, ma'am,' he said, 'you put that shotgun down or I might have to kill your husband.' Flint raised Old Reliable and fired another shot. He aimed halfway between the man and his wife. The wife fired a shot before she was ready and fell back with the kick of the shotgun on to a rocking-chair on the porch.

Wheeler emerged from the shadows with his hands held high, his Winchester still in his right hand. 'All right, Mister,' he said. 'We don't want no more trouble.'

'You don't want trouble, you throw that firestick away and take a couple of steps in this direction.' Flint turned to the woman still gasping in the rocking-chair. 'And you, ma'am, get yourself out of that chair and come out here real slow with your hands held high.'

After a pause the couple came slowly towards him like a massive Punch-and-Judy show.

Flint held Old Reliable on Wheeler and then swung it towards his wife. 'Now Wheeler, I want you to go saddle up your best horse and come back here ready for the trail.'

'Where we going?' Wheeler whined.

'You do what I say, I'll give you that information

when you come back with that horse. And don't try any clever stuff.'

Wheeler glanced hangdog at his wife. 'What about her?'

Flint nodded. 'She stays with me until you come back. You better stock up with grub. It might be a long trip. And remember one thing: no funny tricks. Mrs Wheeler stays with me until we're good and ready.'

Wheeler hesitated a moment longer, but, when Flint gave him a jerk of the head, he moved off sullenly into the saloon.

Flint kept Wheeler slightly ahead of him and the big man rode with his head held down like he was in a sulk. His horse was big and strong and it needed to be.

'What do you aim to do?' Wheeler mumbled.

'Let's think about what you do,' Flint said. 'And this is it: you ride straight for Remarque's hideout. You show me where it is and you do what I tell you. That way, your loving wife is likely to see you again. If not, she gets to fix you a fine funeral and invites all those Navajo Indian friends of yours to come along and do a dance and wail a lament. You got that through your head, Wheeler?'

Wheeler said nothing.

'And remember this,' Flint continued. 'I already lost one son and I don't aim to lose another. You make a damned-fool move, I shoot you right out of that high saddle of yours.'

Wheeler turned his head. 'Listen, Mr Flint, I want you to know something. Remarque and that bunch don't mean nothing to me. They just ride in on me. I don't go along with all that killing and bank robbing. I tell you, I'm a man of peace.'

'Like with the Navajo,' Flint grinned. 'So let's keep it that way, shall we?'

Wheeler rode on as sullenly as before. But not for long.

Flint drew Old Reliable and laid her across the saddle. His old Indian fighting senses were suddenly alive and keen. As he stared ahead, some twenty Indians came into view, strung out in a loose line, one or two of them carrying Winchesters and most toting more antiquated weapons.

'My gawd, that's Indians!' Wheeler gasped. 'Looks like a war party!'

'Apaches,' Flint said. Most of the Apaches were up in the Mescalero agency but you couldn't keep tabs on them all the time.

'What do we do?' Wheeler cried out in panic. 'I can't even shoot. I don't have a gun!'

'You don't need a gun,' Flint said. 'Just as long as you got your scalp on your head you'll be OK.'

These Mescaleros had seen them. They were already circling. Twenty against one man. Wheeler hardly counted, with or without a gun.

'Don't let them see your belly shaking like a jelly,' Flint said. 'Apaches like to see a frightened man. It gives them a kind of pleasure.'

The Apaches had made a full circle now they rode in slowly, boldly, but cautiously on their beautiful mustangs. They came to a halt, watching the two riders and summing them up. It was like in the old days except that Flint wouldn't have let the Comanches come so close.

He raised his palm, open in salute. 'I greet you, men of the Mescalero Apache!' he sang out.

For a long moment none of the Apache braves replied. Flint saw that their faces were painted up, red and ochre and black, as if they were ready for war.

One of the braves turned and muttered to another and a ripple of ribald laughter ran through the warriors, mostly at Wheeler's expense, Flint figured.

The foremost Indian made a chopping motion with his hand and the laughter subsided. He gave an abrupt nod and rode forward a pace or two.

'You ride this way,' he said. 'I am Standing Deer.'

Flint raised his hand again. 'I am Flint, Tom Flint,' he said.

Standing Deer turned his head and muttered something to his nearest companion. They both nodded. Standing Deer turned to Flint again. 'You Flint,' he said. 'I know you, Flint. Many years I hear of you. Your name is among the stars. You are Man of Blood. You kill many of our enemy, the Comanche.'

Flint felt his breath coming more easily. 'I killed a few,' he admitted. That was a long time back.'

The Apache grinned. 'Long time back,' he agreed, 'but you are still one big man. The grandfathers of our people the Tinde still keep you in their hearts.' He placed his hand over his heart. 'Man of Blood, we make camp together. We eat and rest and talk about the old times.'

*

107

Jason Flint was half-conscious long before they reached the cabin in the Bosque Redondo. But he kept himself still and tried to stifle his groans. His head felt as though it had been hit by a railroad locomotive, just as Randolph Remarque had said. He thought he was dead and had been taken, or was being taken, to the great place of misery where the wicked live in eternal pain and fire as a preacher had once described.

When they lifted him down from the horse and carried him none too gently into the tacky old cabin that smelled like a hundred pigs had slept in it for a year, he couldn't stop groaning. But despite the feeling that an Indian tomahawk was stuck in the back of his head, he had the savvy to pretend he was out cold.

Voices came from all round, sounding as though they were disembodied and floating in the air: *We were damned fools to bring him here . . . could be dead come morning . . . should have left him to die in the saloon and give Wheeler the job of burying him or giving him to the coyotes . . . like all those damned Navajo he claims to have killed, eh? Why don't we shoot him now? . . . just another Flint . . . ain't that the truth, Randy? . . . kill him and that just leaves old man Flint to deal with . . . what's old man Flint going to do when he finds out the truth?*

Then Jason heard a softer voice and knew it was Rosa Ramondo. Though she was a witch and he could smell the smoke of her *cigarito,* he felt slightly reassured. Would she go along with his killing? She was rolling his head to one side and examining the wound.

'Not as bad as I thought it was,' she said. 'This one's strong and I guess he'll survive. I guess I might save him for myself.'

That caused a guffaw of raucous laughter which didn't please Remarque. 'Listen, Rosa,' he said. 'I think you forgot something. This here is the son of the son-of-a-bitch who killed our father. You got to remember that.'

'That might be true, Randy, but that's a long time back, in Arkansas, so I hear. You and me were just kids at the time.'

'Matter of honour,' Remarque said. 'An' who killed my daddy has to die. I took my oath on that as soon as I could ride and draw a gun and shoot. That's why we're the Regulators.'

'Better off busting a few more banks,' the man with the deep voice said. 'That way we all get rich and retire pretty damned quick. Go to live in California or some-where.'

'Anyway, how do we aim to use this man-bait to reel Flint in,' the bow-legged man Fielder asked. 'Could be better for me to ride in on the Flint ranch and just pop Flint one in the head like I done to Cassidy. Nothing to it. Then you can breathe easy, Randy.'

'Sure, just like you shot that fool Cassidy,' the deep voice jeered.

'You shouldn't have shot Cassidy like that,' Rosa complained. 'He might have been a fool but he had a lot of good in him.'

'You should know that,' the man with the deep voice rejoined.

The other boys guffawed with laughter.

'That wouldn't figure anyway,' Remarque said. 'I

want to see Flint dying by slow degrees for what he did to my pa.'

There was an awkward pause. 'Didn't I hear it wasn't Flint who killed your pa?' Fielder said mischievously. 'I heard it was Flint's sweet woman Marie who became Flint's wife that fired the shot that killed your pa. Shot him right in the back of the head, so I heard.'

Jason could hear that Remarque was getting riled up. 'That's nothing but lies, Fielder, and you know it. Sure, that woman crept up on Wolf and fired a shot right at him from behind after Wolf and Flint had shot it out.' He paused. 'Wolf would have taken Flint then, as everyone knows. That's why I make sure Flint's wife gets hers just as soon as we kill Flint. Could be we take them both together. That's what I would call justice.'

That caused a buzz of voices, some down to agreement and some of objection.

'Could be we're taking this whole thing a little bit far,' the man with the deep voice said. Jason remembered having seen him: tall and rangy with an Adam's apple that stuck out and wobbled when he spoke as though it might hurt. He might have made a great singer!

'It might be a bit far for you,' Remarque growled, 'but it ain't far enough for me. I shan't rest till I flush out and kill all that damned Flint brood.'

Flint and Standing Deer sat facing one another over a fire the Indians had built against the coming of night. Flint had tied Wheeler's wrists with rawhide so he couldn't make a break for it and get away to warn

110

Remarque that they were on the trail.

'Why do you have to do this to me, Flint?' Wheeler moaned.

'Don't you worry none,' Flint advised him. 'You just hunker down and think about directions. Come sun-up I want us to be right where we can strike Remarque and his buddy boys.'

Standing Deer was watching him close. Obviously he had no opinion of Wheeler who, by his reckoning, was just a big bag of lard, or something worse!

'This man your prisoner, Man of Blood?' he had asked.

Flint had explained, and Standing Deer had listened intently. 'So this man Remarque wishes to kill you and your sons?' the chief asked.

'Thinks it's a matter of honour,' Flint conceded. 'It seems I killed his father way back in the early sixties. So now he's set on killing me.'

Standing Deer nodded his head thoughtfully. "I know this man Remarque,' he said. 'And I know the woman you speak of.'

Flint was chewing on the jack rabbit the Apache had supplied. 'I hear they hole up in the Bosque Redondo?' Flint said.

Standing Deer was nodding and considering again. 'I know the place. Where we live five years with the Navajo.'

Flint narrowed his eyes. 'You mean you know the exact place where those *bandidos* are holed up?'

The chief grinned. 'I know it, Man of Blood.'

Flint paused. He saw Wheeler looking at him from

111

where he lay. 'Maybe you could guide me there, Standing Deer?' he said.

Standing Deer turned the proposal over in his mind. 'I show you, Man of Blood, but I not go there. That place bad medicine, has many bad spirits.' He shrugged his shoulders. 'Not good place for my people. Tomorrow we ride to our place in Mescalero agency. Tinde people not to start war. Man, woman and much children killed.' The chief glanced in the direction of Wheeler who lay close by in a sullen mood. 'But you are my brother, Man of Blood. You help us fight our enemy the Comanche. So I show you where you find this Remarque.'

The chief took a pointed stick and began to trace a map in the dust. He picked out the trail with reference to bluffs and hollows and then drew a circle round an area of dots. This our old village,' he said solemnly, 'but I not go there. And this' – he jabbed a place on the improvised map with his stick – 'this the cabin where Remarque holes up.'

Flint leaned forward to study and memorize the details of the map. 'Any cover round the place?' he asked.

'No cover,' the chief said. 'Only sage and chaparral.' The chief shrugged his shoulders. 'Remarque has many men, Flint. They drink much and eat peyote.' He thumped his chest. 'Peyote good for Tinde man. Helps him to see other world. When bad man eats it he goes mad and wants only to kill.'

That's the truth, Flint thought.

Standing Deer nodded and turned to Wheeler. 'This

man not lead you there,' he said. 'He lead you into the desert so you die.'

'I don't think so,' Flint said. 'He does that, he dies too.'

Standing Deer was grinning. He took out his hunting knife and held it against his throat. 'You don't need this man. You kill him.'

Wheeler groaned. 'Listen, Flint, I got to go. I lie around here, I mess up my pants.'

Standing Deer opened his mouth and laughed.

CHAPTER EIGHT

Marie was restless. She could think of nothing but the fate of her two sons and her husband. And now the callous killing of Sheriff Cassidy! It seemed that the whole world was caving in on her, and she could do nothing to save herself and her kin. That was when she saw Baldy Barlow riding towards the ranch again. Mayor Slocum had been impressed by Baldy's riding. Despite his disability, Baldy sat his horse like he was a born cowpuncher, and now he had acquired a Winchester. When he looked down at Marie, she could hardly think he was the same semi-crippled man who lurched down El Jango's Main Street. His riding skills even seemed to have enhanced his confidence and improved his speech.

'I came back, Mrs Flint,' he said. 'I just had to turn around and leave those mouth bums to theirselves.'

Marie looked at him and, despite her concerns, she couldn't help smiling. 'What can I do for you, Baldy?'

Baldy had on a big floppy hat to hide his baldness and give him stature. 'It's what I can do for you, Mrs

Flint. I want you to know I feel real bad about Sheriff Cassidy, ma'am, the callous way he was shot down like that. And I feel bad about Mr Flint and your son Jason too, ma'am. Soon as I heard about your son Jason and Mr Flint lighting out to find those skookums, I knew I had to help.'

'That's real nice of you, Baldy,' Marie said. Although she was patient with Baldy, like most folks, she didn't think he amounted to much. 'But I don't see what you can do for me.'

Baldy started laughing in a strange high-pitched fashion. 'That's the way most people feel about me, but you know what, Mrs Flint, I see things other folks can't see. They think I'm plumb loco and I play up to their foolishness. You probably don't know this but I'm part Indian – Jicarilla Apache on my mother's side. When you said Jason and then Mr Flint had gone to the Rio Pecos saloon, I knew they were set to get theirselves killed. I know that place and I bin there a few times. Run by a big-mouth called Wheeler who ain't what he seems.'

When Baldy said *I knew they were set to get theirselves killed* Marie's flesh crept and the roots of her hair stood up in horror, but Baldy didn't take note of that; he still had more to say.

'And I think I know where those killers are holed up too, Mrs Flint. The bird of my ancestors came and told me in a dream.'

He spoke with such conviction that Marie began to take him seriously. 'What did the bird say to you, Baldy?' she asked.

115

'This big owl bird came to me and shrieked. It spoke to me like I'm speaking to you now. Said it was one of the grandfathers and it wanted to help. Told me every detail of the place.' Baldy cocked his head on one side just as if he was a bird himself. 'You come along with me, Mrs Flint, I show you the place. Maybe together we can work our how to save your good men.'

Jason was still stretched on the floor of the noxious cabin in the Bosque Redondo. His hands were tied behind his back but he was working to get them lose. He was fully conscious though his head seemed full of a horde of warring scorpions. When he opened his eyes he focused on a woman and knew it was Rosa Ramondo. She was smoking one of her *cigaritos* and staring at him with her big brown eyes.

'So you're awake now?' she said and her voice seemed to echo around, as if there were twenty of her in the cabin.

Jason kept quiet. He didn't want her to know how much he had revived since Fielder had struck down on him with his pistol.

She leaned forward and whispered close to his ear. 'They want to kill you for what your daddy did to our daddy,' she whispered. 'That might sound crazy but it's true. You want for me to save your life?' Rosa judged from the slight shadow that crossed Jason's eyes that he understood. 'All right then,' she whispered again. 'You do what I tell you, you live. You do anything dumb, you die. OK?'

Jason gave a faint, almost imperceptible, nod and she

gave him a cool drink out of a leather bottle – rye and water – which revived him considerably. Then she slid away.

He turned his head slightly and saw there were others in the cabin, slumped in various postures of sleep, some of them snoring like horses.

Earlier he had heard talking, angry and loud. 'I've figured things out,' Remarque said. 'Come sun-up, we ride for the Flint spread. We call old man Flint out and crucify his son right there in front of his eyes.'

The man with the prominent Adam's apple, whose name was Tovey, gave a low chuckle as if he appreciated the joke. 'You can't do that, Randy,' he said. 'It ain't practical.'

'What's practical?' Remarque objected. 'You want to do something, you do it. That's what my old man maintained, or so I'm told. He was the bravest man west of the Mississippi River.'

'That may be so,' Tovey rejoined, 'and I don't blame you none for respecting his memory. But you got to be practical. You take out all those Flints you'll have the whole county on our tails.'

'I don't give a damn for the whole county,' Remarque said in a low menacing growl.

Tovey could hear Remarque was getting riled up but he wasn't about to be put off. 'Consider this, Randy,' he said. 'We got the future to think about. Two more bank busts and we could all retire. Have you thought of that? Better than wasting ammunition and rope on revenge. The boys aren't going to go along with that and neither will Rosa. You got one of those Flints and that's enough.

Rosa might be Wolf's daughter too but she can't remember him none. She was only a few months short of a year when her pa died. And Wolf wasn't much of a good daddy to her anyway from what I hear. Probably wasn't her daddy at all 'cept her ma says so.' He turned to Fielder. 'What's your opinion, Fielder? You don't make no bones about things?'

Fielder laughed in that quiet, sinister tone that was his brand. 'You want to kill Flint and his brood, I don't give a hoot,' he said. 'If it's as easy as pushing off that goofy Sheriff Cassidy I could do it with one arm tied up behind my back. But one thing I do know. This is a real stink hole and I don't aim to stay here any longer than necessary. I want the big bank bust like you, Tovey, so's I can retire and live the life of a respectable bank robber, some place east or California, maybe.'

Tovey laughed like a buffalo snorting. 'You should be so lucky, Fielder.'

Fielder snorted back. 'Come sun-up, I guess I'll ride out and do a bit of looksee on my own. I can't stand this polecat atmosphere in here.'

Fielder went out under the *ramada* and saw the first blush of dawn creeping up over the unwelcoming landscape. Remarque had gone out too. He was squatting on a bench smoking a quirly and looking somewhat thoughtful.

'Thought I'd do myself a patrol,' Fielder said. 'Take a breath of air. Can't stand the stink in that rat hole.'

Remarque chuckled. 'That's OK with me, buddy,' he said. 'We don't have long to wait. Come sun-up we ride. We don't come back here. I got other places in mind.

118

And a patrol could be useful. Don't like the way those Apache Indians have been riding around lately. We see them on the way out, we shoot them up a little and scare the shits out of them.'

'It'll be a pleasure, Randy,' Fielder said with relish. 'I could shoot down one or two before breakfast. Give me an appetite. You know what someone said about Indians: *the only good Indian is a dead Indian.*'

Fielder gathered his palomino from the rail and headed north-east, where he would see the sun riding up to greet him. He would take things kind of easy. But he was worried. He had known Remarque was crazy for some time. It was his craziness had decided to kill Cassidy though he knew Rosa didn't go along with that. Rosa was halfway to being crazy herself but she had held something of a candle for Cassidy even if she had pretended not to. Randy's fanatical determination to rub the Flints right out of the picture made Fielder feel a little prickly, though he had no particular objection to killing in principle. You kill a man if you have to. Bearing a grudge from your childhood was something else again!

Three figures came jogging along through the sage. One was a woman, the second a scrunched man with a twisted back, the third a rather disdainful cowpuncher who hadn't quite worked out the deal. He was Steve Rollins who had said he hated Mexicans and would be happy to see the boy and his father swing from the dead tree.

'You say you know where we're headed?' he said to the scrunched-up rider, who was Baldy Barlow and whom he had always figured as a laughing-stock.

119

Baldy sat low and relentless in the saddle. He might be handicapped and awkward but he seemed to know what he was doing.

'I know the place,' Baldy informed him. 'Knowed it since way back when I was a kid.'

Steve Rollins chuckled to himself. It didn't make no nevermind to him. Riding through the early light was kind of eerie but enjoyable, specially when you didn't know what lay ahead.

'You say Mr Flint and Jason might be in danger,' Rollins said to Marie.

She had been riding with grim determination, like Baldy. She had picked out Steve to ride with them because she knew from past experience that, when Steve took on a task, he liked to go through with it. Also she had heard he was good with a gun. When the boys shot at cans and bottles out by the bunkhouse, Steve usually got the highest score.

'I believe my son and my husband are in considerable danger,' Marie told him.

'I guess that means shooting, Mrs Flint,' Rollins said with a grin.

'There will be shooting, that's for sure,' Baldy said over his shoulder.

Marie rode behind Baldy with some apprehension. What might lie ahead? she wondered.

Flint was still riding slightly behind Wheeler so he could keep him in view. Wheeler had his wrists trussed up together in front of him. He could control his mount but he couldn't make a move to free himself.

'Why don't you cut me loose, Flint? This rawhide is burning into my flesh so deep it's likely to scar me for ever,' Wheeler squealed.

'Good thing to attend to your horse,' Flint said. 'The way she hangs her head, I don't think she cares for you much.'

'That's not funny, Flint,' the big man moaned. 'I nearly got you to where you want to go, didn't I? Can't be more than a mile or two now,' he complained. 'You turn me loose now, I promise I won't make no trouble. When we get over this next rise, you'll see the whole fleabitten outfit before you – all those old Indian shacks. I can pick out the very one you want. Anyways, you'll see by the horses, and the boys will be rustling up chow soon as the sun gets up.'

'I'll think about that,' Flint said. 'You make trouble, I shoot you anyway. That's the deal.'

Wheeler shook his head. 'I go right down there with you, they shoot me. Then I'm dead both ways.'

Even as he spoke Flint saw a movement ahead and to his right He drew Old Reliable and laid her across the saddle as another rider approached from above. A shortish man on a well-tried palomino horse. The man had seen them first and he rode down quite leisurely, as though he was about to greet two old *compadres*.

'Hi there!' he called. 'Why, if it ain't my old friend Wheeler. What brings you this way, Mr Wheeler? And so early in the day too. You should be tending your hens an' all.'

He rode closer and saw that Wheeler had his wrists tied together on the saddle horn.

121

'My, my, Mr Wheeler, you seem to be trussed up somewhat like one of those chickens ready for the oven. How come?'

Wheeler didn't know what to say; he wasn't a quick thinker.

Fielder gave them a sample of his own sinister-sounding cackle. His cool but calculating eye turned to Flint. 'You about to introduce me to your friend, Wheeler?'

Despite the pseudo-friendly talk, Flint saw that the man's hand was playing with the butt of his Colt.

'Name's Flint,' he said.

Fielder's eyes kindled up. 'Ah, Mr Flint, heard about you, quite recently. What brings you here to this god-forsaken country? I'm Fielder, by the way.' Flint saw that Fielder made no move away from the butt of his Colt.

'I heard about you too, Fielder,' he said.

Fielder twitched his thin eyebrows. 'I've been around,' he said in a jeering tone. 'Known pretty well up Las Vegas way. Come to think about it I think I met another Flint recently. Could that be your son? Jason, I think his name was.'

Flint turned his horse to meet the man's jeering gaze. Wheeler was looking back over his shoulder, trying to figure out what might happen next and not feeling too happy about the likely outcome.

Flint spoke in a quiet matter-of-fact tone, as if they were discussing the weather. 'You met my son, you know where he is?' he said.

Fielder grinned and showed a line of crooked teeth. 'I think I can say I do,' he declared. 'Friend of mine's got him tucked away somewheres. Your son met with a slight accident. Sort of collided with the barrel of a gun. I figured he might die but he has a pretty hard head and I think he aims to live . . . a little longer, at least.' Fielder held his head on one side and pushed out a pink tongue. 'Another friend of mine, a real sweet woman, is looking after him. Her name's Rosa, a real nice young woman. Daughter of a man called Wolf. You might have heard of him?' One eyebrow shot up and the lid of his other eye came down in a slow wink.

Flint nodded but betrayed no emotion. 'I believe I did encounter a man called Wolf in the past. A killer, I recall.'

Fielder twitched a finger on the Colt. 'That would be the man,' he said.

'Tell you what you do, Mr Fielder,' Flint said. 'You take me to this place where Rosa is caring for Jason Flint, I'll be greatly obliged.'

Fielder looked thoughtful. 'I have a better plan, Mr Flint. I'll ride with you to where you can see the place. Then we ask Mr Wheeler here to continue on down and announce our arrival. Don't want to give Rosa and Randy too much of a surprise, do we? Could make them kind of twitchy, you know. Randy can be a little quick on the trigger-finger.' Fielder's hand was still on the butt of his Colt. Looked like its habitual position. He stroked it like a loving father.

'I can't go down there,' Wheeler squealed. 'Remarque sees me he'll know I led you here and he'll blow my head off.'

Fielder cackled. 'Don't you worry none, Wheeler. I think he might want to hear what you have to say first,' he said. 'Then he might blow your head off. That's the truth.' He looked thoughtful. 'Tell you what, why don't we cut those thongs on your wrists and make things easier for you. How would that be?' He turned a slanting glance in Flint's direction and gave him the shadow of another wink.

Flint considered the position. Riding along with Wheeler to Remarque's hideaway could be tricky, especially with Fielder at his elbow. So he leaned forward and sliced the rawhide between Wheeler's wrists. Wheeler stopped complaining and rubbed his wrists. He turned to look at Fielder and then at Flint.

'Now you ride on good and gentle and tell Mr Remarque he has a visitor, name of Flint,' Fielder said.

Flint had his eyes on Fielder. He figured it made no difference whether Wheeler rode on or made a dash for cover. One way or the other Remarque would soon know he was coming. Now Fielder would make some kind of move.

Wheeler rode on to the top of the bluff, from were, Flint guessed, you looked down over a rambling collection of sagging buildings where Remarque and his sidekicks were housed.

Flint's attention was divided. He had half an eye on Wheeler, wondering how he would play the situation, and half an eye on Fielder, whom he was still assessing. At that point he didn't know that Fielder had killed Cassidy, but had already gathered that the only thing keeping Fielder from drawing and trying to kill him was that he thought he was saving him for Remarque.

Fielder was eyeing him too, still with his hand close

to the Colt. 'I heard tell they call you Man of Blood,' he said in an almost amiable tone.

'There was some talk about that,' Flint allowed. 'Way back twenty years or so before I grew up.'

'Funny how a reputation sticks,' Fielder said in a conversational tone. 'Man gets in the way of your gun. You shoot him. It follows you around like a label on a carpetbag for ever.'

'Guess you'd know about that,' said Flint.

'You kill a man, nobody's ready to forgive you even if they never met you before,' Fielder added with a grin.

'That could be,' Flint agreed.

'Randy's going to get a real surprise,' Fielder said with some pleasure. 'I think he was expecting to visit with you later today.'

'Save him the trouble,' Flint said drily.

'You're right there,' Fielder said. 'I think it's just about time I took you in with me, kind of introduce you.'

So this is the move, Flint thought.

Fielder turned to Flint with his Colt half-drawn, and saw he was looking down the barrel of Flint's gun.

'I don't think you're going to take me in, Fielder,' Flint said evenly. 'If I go in, I go in by my own choosing.'

Fielder raised his thin eyebrows in faint surprise. 'My, you're quick, Mr Flint. I have to give you credit for that. You may be old but you are certainly quick. Doesn't surprise me those Indians called you Man of Blood.'

'You better believe it,' Flint said. 'We don't have time for diarrhoea of the jawbone, Fielder. Get your hands right up above your head real good so Remarque can see who's the trail-boss here.'

Fielder's eyes narrowed to gimlet points. He paused for a split second; then he raised his hands slowly and held them high. But Flint wasn't fooled. Fielder's eyes had signalled to him what to expect. The hands came down on him in a chopping motion to sweep his gun down and away.

Not quite quick enough, Flint thought as he fired. But quick enough to divert my shot.

Next second Fielder was down on him like a raging mountain lion. Flint could have been knocked right out of the saddle and clawed to pieces before he hit the dust, but he remembered his old Zen master whispering *keep control and stay cool*. He whipped the barrel of his Colt across the back of Fielder's head. Then he brought it down again square. Fielder clawed at Flint and fell between the horses. Flint's horse started to buck and the other horse whinnied with terror and galloped away.

Flint retained his hold on his horse's reins and dismounted quickly. He grabbed Fielder by his gunbelt, twisted him round, and pistol-whipped him again.

'Don't know who pistol-whipped, Jason,' he said hoarsely, 'but this one's for him.'

Fielder was groaning but he was out. He rolled over on to his back and stared blindly up at the spread of dawn in the wide pink and dappled sky.

Flint relieved Fielder of his pistol and hurled it away. 'I could have killed you dead,' he muttered to the unconscious man.

If he had known how Fielder had killed Cassidy, he might have been tempted to do it.

CHAPTER NINE

Randy Remarque was sitting out front of the run-down cabin. He was cleaning his carbine and testing the action. He had already oiled his Frontier Colt and laid it on a log in front of him. Maybe he was thinking about that sweet moment of revenge when he would ride to the Flint spread and smoke out those Flints who had killed his father Wolf. He had never known Wolf except by reputation but he wanted to believe Wolf had been the best gun fighter in the West. Remarque's mother, daughter of a Kansas farmer, had made up wonderful stories about Wolf to compensate for the rough deal she had had both with Wolf and after he left.

After taking his revenge on the Flints Randy would lead the boys up Santa Fe way and to Las Vegas where they would bust a few banks, like Tovey had said, and then retire somewhere quiet and maybe raise a few cattle. Who knew? Or maybe he would go East to New York or somewhere to live it up there.

While he was thinking about this the long streak of Tovey was pacing up and down as though he had some kind of a fire smouldering in the seat of his pants.

'Why don't you set down?' Remarque said. 'You make me feel jumpy lolloping around like that.'

Tovey gave him a funny sidelong glance. 'You sure the boys are going to follow you on this one?' he said. 'I have an uneasy feeling about it.'

Remarque furrowed his brow. 'Follow me on what?' he replied.

'Those Flint killings,' Tovey said. 'Seems kinda unnecessary to me. Sure we had to shoot those two guys got in our way at El Jango. And maybe you had a point wanting Fielder to shoot Cassidy because Cassidy knew too much. That much is clear. And taking out the Flint boy off the stage, that made sense too. But I dunno; I feel kinda uneasy about the rest of the deal.'

Remarque went on ruminating. 'I could have shot Cassidy instead of locking him in his own cells. Fact, the thought of him behind the bars of his own cell and rattling them like a chimpanzee had a touch of humour about it. Anyway, Rosa wouldn't have cared too much for me killing him. You got to remember my ma and Rosa's ma were different. Rosa's ma was Mex. Anyway, taking Cassidy out appealed to Fielder. Made hm feel part of the outfit. You know how Fielder is. Likes to be included.'

Tovey did know how Fielder was and he felt concerned about it. A man who enjoys killing can be a liability in any outfit.

Now three of the boys were gathered round the fire they had built up. Remarque looked over and nodded. He noted that Rosa was still in the cabin, watching over Jason Flint. Could be he should have killed the Flint boy in Wheeler's place. Might have done if Rosa hadn't intervened and Fielder hadn't arrived in time to bop him on the head.

While he was thinking about that, he heard the shot. It came, he calculated, from about a mile away on the other side of the hill.

Tovey looked at Remarque quickly and the boys cooking breakfast at the fire straightened up.

'What's that?' a man called Black Eye asked.

'Sounds like Fielder fired off a round,' Tovey said.

Remarque was on his feet with the Frontier Colt in his hand when he saw the silhouette on the hill.

'That ain't Fielder,' Tovey said, reaching for his gun.

'My God, that looks like Wheeler,' Remarque said.

The immense figure of Wheeler came riding down the hill on his big plodding mare.

'That is Wheeler,' Tovey said in surprise. 'Don't look too good neither.'

Wheeler was so haphazard, so wobbly on the horse, that the boys at the fire were inclined to laugh, but they could see the fear in the advancing figure and they too reached for their guns.

'What's with Wheeler?' someone asked.

Wheeler rode right up to the cabin and reined in. His big horse reared and pranced but he managed to hang on.

'What's happening?' Tovey asked.

'Who fired that shot?' Remarque demanded.

Wheeler was trembling. 'That weren't me, Randy. I didn't see. It might have been Fielder and it might have been Flint.'

At the word *Flint* everyone straightened up completely and reached for his gun.

Wheeler went on trying to explain. He might have been a great talker when he was reciting his exploits with the Navajo Indians back in the sixties but he was a complete blabbermouth when it came to emergencies. 'Flint dropped down on me,' he said. 'Came looking for his son Jason. Come close to killing me and my woman. Mad as hell he was. Made me saddle up and show him the way up here. Got caught by Injuns too. Apaches.'

Remarque's eyes narrowed. 'You mean you led Flint out here?'

'I couldn't do nothing else, Randy,' Wheeler whined. 'He was set to shoot me and my woman. That man is a desperate killer!'

Remarque considered the matter. 'So what's with Fielder?' he asked.

'Fielder rode down on us. I think he meant to kill Flint but maybe Flint got the drop on him.'

'You mean Fielder met you riding in?' Remarque said.

'That's the truth, Randy. Fielder came riding right up on us. He and Flint talked for a bit. Then Flint cut me lose and I rode on to warn you. I didn't see who fired that shot. Could have been Flint or Fielder.'

Remarque was still trying to figure things out. He had in mind to blast Wheeler for leading Flint to the hideaway. But there again, maybe Wheeler had done him a service by delivering Flint to the cabin. If Fielder had shot Flint, all they had to do now was to shoot young

130

Flint. If Flint had shot Fielder, that was a different kettle of fish altogether.

'You sure Flint was alone?' Remarque asked, 'that is, apart from you?'

'Oh, he was alone,' Wheeler explained. 'Leastways, I didn't see nobody else. Flint was alone all right.'

Why should Flint ride right up to the place on his own? As Remarque was considering what to do next, Rosa appeared at the door of the cabin.

'What happened up there?' she asked. She had one of those slim *cigaritos* stuck in the corner of her mouth.

'I think we got Flint,' Remarque said. 'Is that boy tied up safe inside there?'

'Safe enough,' Rose said.

'Well, keep him in your sights,' Remarque said. 'I think we got the whole Flint clan here except for the woman.'

Rosa took out her *cigarito* and made to speak but Tovey pointed at the brow of the hill where Wheeler had appeared.

'There's someone riding in,' he drawled, 'and it don't look like Fielder to me.'

The others shaded their eyes. Black Eye said, 'That sure ain't Fielder. Must be Flint.'

'That's Flint for sure,' Wheeler advised. 'Must have shot Fielder.'

A stunned and wary silence fell over the bunch. So this was Tom Flint, so called Man of Blood, whom Remarque hated so much.

'Don't look much to me,' Tovey said. 'Kind of small to what I expected.'

'He's big enough,' Rosa said. Then she disappeared inside the cabin.

Flint came riding slow and easy on his horse and trailing Fielder's palomino behind him. Like Tovey had said, he didn't look like a man to be wary of . . . not until you saw the steel in his eyes and the determined set of his jaw.

'You want me to bring him down?' Black Eye said. 'Could do it easy from here with a well-placed long shot.'

'I don't think so,' Remarque snarled out of the corner of his mouth. 'This one's for me. Don't want to waste him.'

Flint looked down on the sprawl of half-dilapidated cabins and thought about his position. Somewhere down there Jason his son was being held captive.

He took in the bunch of men cooking up breakfast by the fire. He saw Wheeler prancing about on his big horse and trying to control it. He saw Remarque and Tovey standing together and looking up at him with their guns drawn. Even at that distance he recognized Remarque from the picture Cassidy had drawn. He also noted that there was no sign of his son Jason. That grieved him, because he figured Jason might already be dead.

At that distance he could have drawn Old Reliable, his Sharps rifle, and taken a shot at Remarque. He could, perhaps, have picked off Remarque with a single shot if Remarque had obliged him by standing still. Something about the way Remarque half-stooped like a

132

cat ready to spring reminded Flint of Remarque's father, the killer Wolf, who had caused him so much grief back in Arkansas.

Flint knew he was facing a difficult situation. Those men by the fire were the men who had robbed the bank in El Jango and killed his son, Tom junior. And he was on his own. In that position you either turn tail or look for the best advantage.

He remembered the old Zen master who had taught him how to tackle a man who was bigger and stronger than you, as well as a lot of other things like keeping a cool head and searching for a weakness in your opponent. At the moment there was no obvious weakness except, perhaps, in the fat man with the blabber-mouth, Wheeler.

Now Wheeler was looking up at him with the fear of impending death in his eyes. He managed to slide off the big horse and stand with it between them, peering at Flint over the horse's shoulder.

Flint's eyes roamed over the rest of the bunch. He saw Tovey sway slightly away from Remarque, though he still held his carbine ready. The men by the fire were spreading out as though they knew breakfast would have to be delayed somewhat.

Flint's eyes went back to Remarque who seemed to be grinning as if he was pleased that the situation had moved so decisively in his favour.

'So you're Tom Flint,' Remarque said smugly.

'So I'm Tom Flint,' Flint agreed. He reined in and let his horse amble a little. 'And I presume you're Randolph Remarque.'

'And I guess you come in to powwow,' Remarque jeered.

They say that when you're still figuring a situation talking can help. So Flint continued figuring things out as he talked on. 'So who makes the first move?' he asked.

'I guess you already made it,' Remarque said still with the jeering grin on his face. 'They tell me you used to talk with your gun. But you're a little old for that now, Flint, so I guess you're a little slower on the trigger than you used to be when you shot my pa.'

Flint tossed his head. 'I can still shoot a rattlesnake when I see one. And I see one good and clear when I meet one.'

That caused a ripple among Remarque's buddies. Not exactly laughter and not precisely fear, but a kind of high-strung alertness.

'We heard a shot,' Tovey intervened. 'That mean you killed Fielder?'

Flint glanced at the tall stringy man holding the Winchester. 'I don't think I killed Fielder, not so far,' he said. 'He just felt a tap on the head with the barrel of my shooter. It seems it disagreed with him. Right now he's crawling around like a bumblebee with a sore head. I think he'll probably survive.'

That seemed to ease the tone a little. Remarque laughed and the rest of the bunch joined in.

'Might still have some sting left,' Remarque said. 'We all got our stings, Flint. So you managed to persuade Mr Wheeler to show you the way up here? That was real civil of Mr Wheeler. So what exactly can I do for you?'

134

Flint allowed his horse to amble a little more, but not too close to the cabin.

'Figured I'd come to enquire about my son, Jason,' he said.

Remarque nodded. That seemed to puzzle him. He was scratching his chin and looking thoughtful. 'I think I can enlighten you about that,' he said. 'In fact, we got Jason tucked up real good. Got a slight bump on the head like Fielder, but has shown signs of improvement, I believe. Rosa's caring for him right now. But I don't think he's well enough to receive visitors yet.'

Like a patient in an infirmary, Flint thought.

'Maybe the nurse should ask him,' he said.

Remarque nodded and grinned again. He was playing his cards really cool. He half-turned his head towards the boys round the fire. 'Why don't two of you boys bring the kid out here. Me and Mr Flint need to talk a little turkey.'

That cleared up one thing for Flint. At least Jason was still alive. Black Eye and another of the men disappeared into the cabin and, after a moment, brought the prisoner out.

Jason stood between the two men with his hands apparently tied behind his back. Rosa sidled out too with a *cigarito* in the corner of her mouth. Flint caught the gleam of her eyes at once as she stared unflinchingly at him. So this was the woman who had betrayed Cassidy and led him to make a fool of himself.

But mainly he was looking at his son Jason. And Jason, standing between the two gunslingers, looked forlorn and hung down with the bandages on his head.

135

'You see, Flint, we got your son done up real good. I guess he'll be right glad to greet you, 'Remarque said.

Jason raised his head and met his father's eye. It was only a momentary glance but it told Flint a lot. Jason might be hurt but he was burning up with fury at being caught like that. The fire in his eyes told Flint he still had lot of fight left in him.

Flint nodded and thought, this is the crunch line. This is the moment of truth.

'Now, I'm about to make a suggestion to you,' Remarque drawled out. 'This is the big deal. You want your son, we give him to you. We don't have time to keep him around here anyway. You drop your long gun and throw that Colt away. Then you dismount and walk a little closer with your hands raised above your head. We bring Jason out halfway to meet you. You and your boy shake hands. Jason mounts up and rides away and you come on in to join with us.'

Flint knew that was a bum deal and would never come to reality. As soon as he and Jason met and shook they would be like dummies begging to be shot down by an execution squad.

'What's the next scene?' he asked between clenched teeth.

Remarque stood with his legs apart looking smug. 'That's the best deal I can offer you, Flint,' he said. 'A son for a father, father for a son. Just like the good book says: *An eye for an eye and a tooth for a tooth.* Seems a good deal to me.'

Flint nodded. 'I get the picture,' he said. 'I get it real good. But I have a better deal to offer and this is it: you let Jason walk right out to meet me. He mounts up. We ride away together. You go on cooking up breakfast. That way nobody gets hurt.'

Remarque swayed a little and began to chuckle. 'That's a fairytale ending, Flint, and you know it. That's not going to happen. You got all the wrong cards, man.' He raised his Winchester to emphasize the fact that he held all the good cards, including the aces, up his sleeve.

Flint caught a flash of the old Zen master again. When you're dead, you're dead. So, when you're alive, keep talking and still look for a fatal weakness in the adversary. Then you know how to act.

Except that so far he couldn't see a weakness.

'We play it your way, Remarque,' he said, 'a lot of people are liable to get killed. I hope you see that. Dead men eat no breakfast. That applies to dinner too.'

As he spoke his son Jason raised his head again and briefly looked his father in the eye. Flint knew he was trying to make a signal but he couldn't yet figure what.

Flint knew something had to give . . . and something did give. Rosa suddenly snapped the *cigarito* out of the corner of her mouth and said: 'Like the man said, someone is liable to get killed, Randy. I say we turn Jason loose. Nobody is going to win in this deal. Not you, not Flint.'

It was as though someone had struck Remarque in the middle of his forehead. His head jerked back and a look of fury distorted his features. 'What the hell?' he raved. 'You gone soft in the head or something?' He half-turned towards Rosa with the Winchester raised.

'Either we kill this hell-raising Comanche-shooter to avenge our father, or he shoots us. Don't you savvy that?'

A look of resignation crossed Rosa's dark features. 'I don't buy that, Randy. And I don't go for that killing. And I don't aim to let you do it.'

Now Remarque almost fell back with astonishment. 'Why, you stupid bitch!' he cried in a high piercing tone of disbelief. Black Eye and the boys by the fire turned to stare at Rosa in amazement. Tovey gripped his carbine as though he was looking for somewhere to loose off a shot.

Everything was moving so quickly. Flint was still trying to read the situation. He saw Remarque was temporarily off guard. He figured if he took a snap shot he could take out the man, but that might risk wounding Jason . . . the last thing he wanted.

Then Rosa spoke again, this time in a harsh and breathless voice. 'I say there's been enough killing,' she repeated, and suddenly a small derringer appeared in her hand. Flint knew that derringer might be small but it was also deadly, especially at close quarters.

The fury of hell seemed to burst like a dam in Remarque. He swung towards his half-sister and fired a shot. It caught her full and blasted her back so that she fell against the door of the cabin and slid down the post to the ground. Black Eye and the other hardcases drew back in horror.

Then Flint saw what his son Jason had been trying to signal to him, that Rosa had untied his hands. Jason sprang at Remarque, thrust his Winchester aside, and went to seize him by the throat. But Remarque was no rookie. He still had the Winchester in his hand and he brought it in with a savage jab to Jason's chest. Then he swung it at Jason and fired a shot. Jason sprang back and keeled over backwards.

That surged right through Flint like poison in his blood. He raised Old Reliable and fired a quick shot at Remarque. Remarque sprang back . . . but did he fall?

Wheeler's big horse suddenly started to rear and buck, carrying the immense bulk of Wheeler off the ground and swinging him out like a rat on a string.

The gunmen by the fire sprang to life and started shooting at Flint. Tovey ran forward and, crouching like an ungainly giraffe, he took a bead on Flint. But the adrenaline was pumping and Flint took a snap shot at the tall man. Tovey flung his gun in the air and fell back against the wall of the cabin. Flint knew he was dead and he swung back to Remarque . . . but there was no sign of Remarque. In an instant he had disappeared round the corner of the cabin under cover of Wheeler's prancing horse.

Next instant, Black Eye and the other gunmen were all loosing off at Flint at the same time as he pulled his horse round this way and that to avoid their fire.

Then a strange, unnerving thing happened. Suddenly from the surrounding ridges there came a wailing sound like the cry of a banshee. High and terrifying enough to freeze the blood, it echoed and swelled, rose and fell, and died away. After a second it rose again, mournful and shrill, before dying away into an eerie silence.

The weird cry had a strange paralysing effect on the

gunmen by the fire, and in an instant they stopped shooting, the hairs on the backs of their necks bristled up straight, and they took on the appearance of men turned to stone.

'What the hell was that?' Black Eye said.

'That's them devil Injuns,' another of the men exclaimed. 'They put a jinx on the place! Now they're coming in to take us off to the bad place!'

Flint was pulling his mount round in a wide circle when he looked up and saw the three riders galloping down the bluff. Some of the Apaches he had met earlier, maybe. Then he knew who they were: Marie, from the way she rode; the bunched-up figure of Baldy Barlow spurring his horse like a madman from hell towards the cabin, and another figure he recognized as Steve Rollins, one of his cowpunchers. Baldy Barlow let out a bloodcurdling shriek as he rode, and Flint guessed he must have been responsible for the weird cries from the ridge.

Baldy Barlow's eerie war cry had had the necessary effect on the so-called Regulators, just enough to turn the tide against them. The man who said *now they're coming to take us off to the bad place* spoke for the whole bunch. The Regulators had stopped shooting and were retreating in some disorder to the corral back of the cabin.

Wheeler had now dropped down from his horse; he was on his back, struggling like a crab to turn himself round. 'My gawd!' he cried. 'Don't let those damned Navajo get their damned hands on me.'

Flint dismounted and ran forward with his Colt in his hand. The first thing on his mind was Jason. He dropped down on one knee and reached out to his son.

Jason lay with his back propped against the cabin and there was blood on his chest and soaking through his shirt. But his eyes flickered towards his father and he struggled to speak. Thank God he was alive.

'Rest up,' Flint said. 'Let me look at that wound.'

Remarque's bullet had caught him high on the chest ripping through the muscle. Maybe the shoulder blade was shattered but it seemed that with care the boy would probably live.

As Flint crouched over his son he heard horses galloping close and almost immediately Marie was by his side, nursing her son. She had witnessed killings and seen much bloodshed, and she wasn't the woman to make a deal of unnecessary fuss. She was already ripping away Jason's shirt and attempting to stem the flow of blood. Jason's eyes rolled towards her and he attempted to smile. Marie had the cork of a bottle between her teeth; she drew it out and applied whiskey to the wound high in Jason's chest.

Jason winced with pain but did not cry out. 'How bad is it?' he gasped.

'You're going to be all right,' Marie said. 'But you got to take things easy, stop the bleeding.'

Jason fought for words. 'Look to Rosa,' he said hoarsely. 'See if she's going to be OK.'

Flint had already switched his attention to Rosa Ramondo. As he bent over her, her eyes came into focus and she struggled to speak. 'Will the kid be all right?' she asked.

'Jason's going to be OK,' Flint said.

But it was too late for Rosa. She was struggling to smile but was losing the battle. Then she tried to speak. Flint bent closer to read her lips.

'It ... should ... have ... been ... different,' she managed to say. Then her eyes rolled back and she died.

Flint looked back over his shoulder and saw the two mounted figures. One was Steve Rollins; the other was Baldly Barlow, hunched over his saddle like a gnome from a Grimm's fairy tale.

'It looks like they gorn, Mr Flint,' Baldy said in his slurred tones.

'Rode off like bats out of hell,' Steve confirmed.

'Want us to go after them and cut them down?' Baldy asked.

Flint immediately straightened up. In his anxiety about Jason he had forgotten about Randolph Remarque and the fact that he'd ridden away. 'You see which way they went?' he asked.

'Rode off in a bunch,' Baldy said. 'All but the leader. He rode on ahead of the others in a different direction. I'll show you where, Mr Flint. I ride along with you and we bring him in together.'

Flint was already in the saddle. 'I don't need you to do that, Baldy,' he said. 'What I want is for you to tidy things up here.' He pointed back over the hill. 'The man called Fielder is over there somewhere. Maybe you could bring him in. He needs to go to trial for killing

Sheriff Cassidy. But take good care. I threw his gun away but he might have found it. He's a cold-blooded killer. So make sure he's tied up like a hog.'

'Sure thing, Mr Flint.' Steve Rollins grinned and gave a kind of half-military salute.

'He tries anything tricky, gun down on him like you would a rattlesnake.'

The two men wheeled their horses and rode for the top of the hill.

'What do I do, Mr Flint?' It was Wheeler's voice. He had managed to roll over somehow, and he was standing shaking like a man who has been doused with ice-cold water.

Flint turned to look down at him with something close to contempt. 'What you do, Wheeler, is you remember all you've witnessed this day. You come before the court you can tell what Remarque did to my boy, and the rest of it . . .'

Wheeler nodded vigorously. 'I'll do that, Mr Flint. I promise you. I swear I never took part in any of those bad things. I'm right glad those desperate men are about to meet their doom.'

Flint unhitched his lariat and snaked it out so that it fell over Wheeler's shoulders. He pulled Wheeler in like a big fish on the end of a line. He dismounted and in a few deft movements trussed him up so he couldn't make any dumb moves.

'There's no need for that,' squealed the big man. 'I ain't going to do nothing. I'm on your side, sir. Those desperate men need to be tamed and strung up.'

Flint was securing the lariat to a post. 'Just making

sure,' he said. 'A man needs to be reminded of his responsibilities from time to time.'

Flint mounted up again. He knew roughly in which direction Remarque had ridden and, from the tracks he picked up, he saw that Remarque had been in a particular hurry. He might be winged but he wouldn't be wounded badly enough to hold him up.

As Flint rode, he thought of Jason lying back there at the cabin with the blood bubbling from the wound in his chest. A quick inspection had told Flint that his son would probably live. But you could never be certain. Then he thought of Tom junior, strung up and dead on the broken tree after the stage hold-up. His mind went back to the bank bust in El Jango and the two men who had been gunned down in cold blood. Then the merciless killing of Cassidy. Maybe Fielder had been the killer, but it all came down to Randolph Remarque, Wolf's son, the man who was fleeing before him.

As he rode the landscape was closing in around him. The ground was strewn with boulders. Yet he could see from the way Remarque was riding his horse, that he was galloping with a recklessness that no horse could sustain. Then he saw where the horse had stumbled and gone lame and he knew Remarque couldn't go on much longer.

Almost before he expected it he came upon the injured horse, hopping and blowing, and attempting to graze among the mesquite. Remarque couldn't be far away. He had just had time to get clear from the horse and struggle into a crevice up on the rock-strewn hill somewhere.

Even as Flint looked up and scanned the bush above, a shot was fired. Close, Flint thought, but not quite close enough. He dismounted and tethered his mount to a mesquite. 'Steady, old buddy. Wait for me here.' An optimistic thought!

'Guessed you wouldn't have the sense to keep back, Flint.' The voice came from above and slightly to the right. It was difficult to pin-point where.

Flint moved quickly from bush to bush, keeping his weapon high. 'I'm going to take you in,' he said. 'Make sure they hang you good from the highest tree, Remarque.'

There was a hoarse laugh. 'That so? I doubt it. You ain't the man you were. Too long in the tooth and too slow. I figure the rheumatics should be gnawing at your bones by now. Why don't you go home for your stick and your rocking-chair?'

Flint ducked low and searched the boulder-strewn hill above. 'You do too much figuring and your tongue is loose enough to fall off,' he said. 'And your brain is a little short on thinking power.' He wormed his way forward to a better position. 'I guess you know you killed your half-sister Rosa back there.'

There was a momentary pause. Just enough to tell Flint he had made Remarque think.

'Rosa had it coming,' he said. 'If she hadn't betrayed me and turned your son loose and pulled that derringer on me like a traitorous bitch, she might have lived. Anyways, I guess you must have noticed I got your

145

son Jason too.'

'You tried,' Flint said. 'That's one good reason I'm here. Except you didn't kill Jason. You got him in the chest. But he will live.'

Another silence, this time slightly longer. Remarque must be thinking back and trying to picture where his bullet had struck Jason.

'You come an inch or two closer, I'm going to kill you, Flint, and that's enough for me. Wipe the slate clean between us. I'm looking forward to that.'

'Don't look too far ahead, Remarque, because I'm coming to get you like I said.' He edged forward a little closer to where the voice was coming from. Difficult to locate. A little to the right or a little to the left of that big red rock?

The sun was getting up high now, roasting the two of them out. Flint figured Remarque wouldn't have a canteen or any water. In short order he would begin to get more than a little thirsty, and that could affect his judgement.

Flint crouched down behind a mesquite sprouting between loose boulders and checked his Colt. Five rounds and maybe another ten in his gunbelt: more than enough to flush out a skunk like Remarque. Old Reliable was back with the horse. But, anyway, a Colt was more useful at close range in this sort of country.

When you're in a situation like this you try to put yourself into the mind of the other man. Remarque would be squatting behind his red rock up there wondering where his adversary was and whether he could pull a surprise move to gun down on him.

146

Remarque might figure Flint was too old and stiff in the joints to move fast. If he could slither away fast enough like a rattlesnake he might even make it to the grazing horse and break away. It could be worth a try.

Flint looked back to where the two horses were grazing. Remarque's crippled mount was whinnying pitifully. There was a deal of cover and Remarque might figure he could just make it.

He heard Remarque clear his throat and knew he was about to speak. 'You sleeping down there?' Remarque said in a hoarse, parched-sounding voice.

Flint said nothing. He raised his head very slightly to watch. The more Remarque spoke, the more likely he would be to give away his position.

Silence, except for a slight breeze that stirred in the valley like the harsh breath of a man waiting for his doomsday.

A slight rustling from above. Like a jackrabbit grazing, stopping to watch and listen.

'How you doin', Flint? Did you pass out from old age or something?'

Still silence from Flint, though he was tempted to laugh.

Remarque coughed quietly. 'You want to shoot it out, Flint? Me against you, the man who killed my father.' His voice sounded different. Did it betray a slight decline in confidence?

Flint had been concentrating, listening, and moving his head slightly to locate where the voice was coming from. Up to the left, he figured, from where the bluff tumbled away in a drift of rocks and scrub to where the

147

horses grazed.

Flint waited until Remarque spoke again.

'You shit scared or something?' Remarque's voice said from behind the big rock.

Flint crept up, Indian fashion, to where he saw Remarque must have climbed to reach the red rock.

They were very close now. Flint could hear Remarque's hoarse breathing. Was it with fear or exertion?

Flint lay just below the rock with the Colt in his hand. A small stone came over the rock and bounced away behind him. A diversionary tactic. He raised his head slowly, just in time to meet Remarque's gaze behind the rock. Both fired in the same moment, though Flint knew neither of them could make a hit.

He heard Remarque scramble away and run. He was making for the horses as Flint had figured. Flint hauled himself up so he could look over the big rock. He saw Remarque zigzagging between the mesquite, down towards the horses. With Old Reliable he could have taken a bead on him and brought him down.

He slithered down the way he had come.

Remarque swivelled and threw a couple of wild shots. Both went wide and Flint heard them ricocheting among the rocks.

Flint was on his feet, running and scrambling for the horses. Remarque was fast. He had reached the crippled horse. Using it as cover, he fired off another two shots in Flint's direction. But the horse spooked, lurched to one side and hurled Remarque on to the ground. His gun went spinning away into the scrub.

Flint ran with his Colt held high. As he drew close Remarque sprang to retrieve his weapon, but changed his mind. He had seen Old Reliable in its saddle holster. He could either try to wrench it free or mount up or ride away like hell.

Maybe he estimated he could do both.

Though Flint was old, he had kept his wind. He could have stood and probably taken Remarque out with a single shot. But he ran forward and seized Remarque by his fustian.

Remarque rolled over and struggled to his feet. Now Flint could have pistol-whipped or shot him. But he preferred another method.

The two men staggered for a moment getting their breath. Then the younger man came in roaring. He seized Flint high on the jacket and might have head-butted him or forced him down. But Flint worked by instinct – an instinct that had been fine-tuned by his Zen master. He rolled back with his foot above Remarque's crotch and flipped back in a *tomoenage* stomach throw. The ground was hard but it was a lot harder for Remarque.

Remarque lay on his back, gasping to get the air into his lungs. But Flint didn't waste time. The adrenaline pumped through his veins and he sprang round to face the killer.

Remarque was struggling to his feet when Flint's boot caught him on the side of the jaw and threw him back. But Remarque wasn't finished. He had the strength of a desperate man and he struggled up again, wiping the blood off his face with the back of his hand.

149

Now it was time for fists. Flint moved in quickly, pumping into Remarque's body and face. 'That one's for Tom, and that one's for Jason, and that one's for Cassidy, and the rest,' he gasped. One, two, three, four!

Remarque sprawled back and lay with his arms spread. He was still conscious, but he had clearly had more than enough.

Flint retrieved his Colt, cocked it, and levelled it at Remarque's head.

'I should shoot you and bring your miserable life to an end,' he said hoarsely. 'But I'm going to leave that to the judge and the hangman. So get yourself up on your feet and move.'

At that moment, Baldy Barlow rode up, sitting low in the saddle. He peered down at Remarque's supine body with contempt. 'See you got him, Mr Flint,' he said.

CHAPTER TEN

'Funny thing about Fielder,' Chisum said.

Flint looked up from his plate of rare steak and beans and regarded the rancher with an air of grave concern. 'Not so funny by my book,' he said.

Chisum grinned and shrugged. 'Well, you know, not funny so much as funny. You know what I mean?'

The two men were sitting in Frenchy's and Frenchy was watching them from behind the counter. He had secret ambitions to write about the famous men of the West and their exploits. So when he saw Flint coming in through the door he pulled out the secret pad he kept and made sure his pencil was good and sharp. He had already heard from Baldy Barlow on the subject of Fielder but he wanted Flint's take on the subject. But before he could seize the moment and ask his question, the door of Frenchy's diner was thrown open and the reporter Pike Willcox sprang into the room. He was carrying his notepad and flourishing a pencil.

'Ah, Mr Flint,' he crowed. 'Caught you at last! Mind if I ask you a few questions about recent events, how you rounded up those self-styled Regulators and brought them in. Then maybe you would be kind enough to step over to my studio so I could take a portrait. Official, you know, for the *Las Vegas Gazette*.'

Flint placed his fork precisely on his plate and gave Willcox a hard stare. 'As you may have noticed,' he said, 'I happen at this moment to be pitching into one of Frenchy's juicy steaks.'

Willcox paused. 'Oh, yes, I see what you mean. I wouldn't like to take a brave man away from his victuals, eh?' He gave a nervous giggle. 'I just know those folk all round the territory and even back East would like to know exactly what happened up there in the Bosque Redondo. And what your secret is.'

At the mention of a brave man, Chisum gave a slight chuckle of derision. He had no great belief in brave men. A man had to do what he had to do and that was enough.

Flint glanced over at Frenchy. 'Ask Baldy Barlow,' he said. 'He'll give you the lowdown on everything. If it hadn't been for Baldy's ghost impressions those killers might have gunned down on us all. Don't know where he learned those yodelling tricks but they sure enough worked. And that put those hoodlums at some disadvantage.'

'Thank you, Mr Flint,' the reporter said. 'I'll catch up with you later, and if you would be kind enough . . .'

Flint nodded briskly. 'When I finished my chow, I'll step across the street and face that infernal flash machine you got.'

'Oh, thanks again, Mr Flint.' Willcox bowed almost to the ground and went to engage Baldy Barlow, who had just emerged from somewhere back of Frenchy's, munching one of Frenchy's special cookies. Baldy had gained great credit for his ghosty intervention in the shoot-out in the Bosque Redondo and most of the people who had previously thought he was stupid now conceded he had special powers.

When they had disappeared behind the counter with Frenchy listening eagerly to the conversation, Chisum wiped his mouth with the back of his hand and let forth a somewhat immodest belch.

'So, how's the boy?' he asked.

Flint nodded thoughtfully. 'Jason's recovering. That was a bad wound in his shoulder but with good care from his mother he's going to be OK. He's itching to get back into the saddle again. Feels he let me down over that whole business. But, like I told him, if he hadn't gone off to the Wheeler place like that, those killers would still be prowling around the range, waiting behind every rock to gun down on us. So Jason did good and he'll learn. That's the main thing.'

Chisum shook his sceptical head. 'Jason's got good blood running in his veins from both you and his mother. Marie's a fine woman.' He knew he could have done more to help Flint. So he felt somewhat embarrassed. 'I guess the boy won't be nowhere fit for round-up and the drive north,' he surmised.

'That's as maybe,' Flint conceded. 'Marie is against it but Jason's headstrong. So I guess he might come along even if it's only for the ride.'

Chisum leaned forward, elbows on the table. 'I want

153

you to know, I'll do all I can to help you out in these difficult times.'

Flint grinned. 'I know you been busy, John, but I appreciate your consideration.'

He got up from the table and went over to pay his bill. Frenchy felt inclined to say 'This is on the house' but he had a wife and children to consider and times, as usual, were hard.

As Flint raked in his change and stowed it in the back pocket of his britches, Frenchy leaned forward eagerly. 'Don't mind me asking, Mr Flint, I never did catch up on what happened to that desperado Fielder. Heard Mr Chisum mention it but I don't believe you gave an answer.'

Now Chisum was on his feet, approaching the counter. 'Funny thing about Fielder,' he said again. 'Seems nobody knows the answer.'

Frenchy had pulled out his pad and pencil ready to scribble. 'This is for the book I hope to write some day,' he said with a degree of modesty. 'They do say every man has a book in him somewhere and this is going to be mine.'

'So you aim for us to make you famous?' Flint grinned.

'Well. . . ?' Frenchy gave a modest shrug . . . 'maybe it's only a pipe dream, but they do tell me Governor Wallace is writing a piece about Roman slaves or some-thing.'

'I guess that's why we don't see much of him,' Chisum said in disgust.

Frenchy laughed somewhat over-heartily.

'Tell you the truth I can't answer your question about

Fielder,' Flint said. 'Only to say when I left him back there he was out cold. Nobody's seen him since. I don't know what happened but I can guess.'

One thing everyone knew. The authorities had put up Wanted notices depicting Fielder all over the county and beyond. Chisum himself had given a deal of money to have him brought in.

'Sure,' Frenchy said, wielding his pencil. 'Go ahead, Mr Flint. Tell me what you think happened.'

'Yes. I'd like to hear your guess,' Chisum said.

Flint ruminated quietly for a moment. 'Put yourself in Fielder's head,' he said. 'He comes round. He wonders what's hit him. Might think for a second he's been shot. He can't remember exactly. Then it starts to come back. An old geek he thinks he can shoot down or get the drop on, tumbles him off his horse and pistol-whips him. Now he has no horse and no gun. A man like Fielder without a gun feels like a naked swimmer who finds someone stole his pants. So he shakes his head and groans and walks with some difficulty to the top of the hill. He looks down and sees what's happening – Wheeler swinging like a bloated ape from his horse, Tovey pitching back with a bullet in his head, Remarque killing Rosa – and he sees there's no glory in it for him any more. So what does he do? He decides to protect his skin. He makes a tactical withdrawal. Baldy Barlow and Rollins ride up looking for him. But the man wants to be remembered as a killer, not as a tame pig led by a ring in his nose. So he slides away into the bush like a rattlesnake and disappears.'

Frenchy was scribbling on his pad so fast his pencil

155

was almost taking fire. '*Like a pig with a ring in his nose.* I like that, Mr Flint. It has style, you know that?'

Chisum gave Flint a sceptical look. 'That your theory?'

'That's my theory,' Flint said.

'You think Fielder could survive out there?' Frenchy asked him.

Flint considered the matter. 'That's an interesting question. We don't know much about Fielder, except for his love of killing. He might have Apache friends but I doubt it. Indians usually have a sense of honour and I don't think they'd care for Fielder's manner too much. So he could die and he could live. Could go either way. Depends on the circumstances.'

'And if he lives?' Chisum asked.

Flint shrugged. 'He lives, he lives. Keeps his head down and gets clear of the territory for a time. Grows a beard or a *mustachio.* Goes to Mexico or California, maybe, even as far as Canada. Sees it's time to change his name. Hires himself out as a gun. Only trade he knows is shooting men down in cold blood. Fielder is a killer and, even if he's lying out there somewhere being eaten by coyotes or grizzlies, he will still be a killer.'

'So that's your theory?' Frenchy said eagerly. He scribbled the word *mustachio* on his pad, thinking that had style too.

'That's what I think,' Flint said.

They put Remarque on trial in Santa Fe. A United States deputy marshal rode down to El Jango, where Remarque was being held in the town jail. Pike Willcox wanted to take his picture with his newfangled camera, but the deputy marshal, name of Smith, wouldn't allow it. He was a stone-faced *hombre*, a friend of Pat Garrett, the man who had gunned down the Kid, and he always dealt his cards from the top of the deck.

Biggest thing since the death of the Kid, some reckoned. Everyone who could went up for the trial and it caused a minor boom in the town of Santa Fe. Knowing how slippery Remarque was and how the Kid had escaped from custody, they kept a twenty-four-hour watch on the jail.

Guilty of killing his half-sister Rosa Ramondo and of attempting to kill Jason Flint. They couldn't pin the murder of Jim Stacey or Jerry, the bank teller on him, or the cruel murder of Tom Flint junior since there were no reliable witnesses. But the jury and the judge were satisfied and Remarque was sentenced to be hanged.

When sentence was pronounced, Remarque stood like a man carved out of stone in the dock. He stared across at Flint and his face was white as chalk.

'Does the guilty man have anything to say?' the judge droned as a matter of form.

Remarque took a sip of water and ran his tongue along his lower lip. 'Just one thing,' he said hoarsely, 'and that's for Flint. I could have killed you, Flint. I could have shot you from ambush. I had plenty of chances. But I saved you because I wanted to see you suffer.' His mouth twisted in a grin. 'And I made you suffer, Flint, I made you suffer.' At that moment, Flint felt as though someone had walked on his grave . . . and that someone was the man called Wolf!

Flint watched them take the condemned man out to the cells and, at the last second, Remarque looked back over his shoulder. 'When I swing, Flint,' he snarled, 'you'll swing with me. I mean to rise from the dead and put a curse on you.'

He went out with such a sinister laugh that even the judge turned a pale shade of grey.

'How did you feel about that?' Chisum asked Flint.

Flint considered matters for a second or two. 'I didn't feel a thing,' he said. 'Marie felt something. I think she almost fainted in court, but she held herself together like the brave girl she is. But I didn't attach any importance to that cursing because I don't buy all that superstitious nonsense about men rising from the grave to haunt their enemies.' He paused a moment. 'Any road, I figured Remarque had no case against me. So the idea of haunting was a matter of moonshine.' He paused again. 'But I did notice one thing: that guy Wheeler who claimed to have fought with Kit Carson to subdue the Navajo. He had a fit of coughing. So they had to carry him from the courthouse. It took six men. So that was no small deal.'

There was no attempt to spring Remarque out of jail. The rest of the so-called Regulators had dispersed like smoke among the hills. Flint knew they might get themselves together, maybe in Mexico, or Arizona, and make a nuisance of themselves, but he figured they would steer well clear of him. Who could tell?

The morning they hanged Remarque the sun hung like a poached egg in a slate-grey sky. They said he tried to speak before they pulled the lever, but he was half a second too late.

Flint was on the range herding his steers up north along the Goodnight–Loving Trail to Cheyenne. Steve Rollins was cussing as usual but he buttoned his tongue when he saw the hunched-up figure of Baldy Barlow riding up beside him. Baldy was there because he wanted to be there. He would never be great shakes as a cowpuncher but he rode well and had an unexpectedly fine tenor voice when he sang to the boys come sundown. Despite his obvious handicaps, because of the way he stormed down on the skookums at the cabin in the Bosque Redondo, everyone respected him.

Hanging close by Flint on the trail was the small figure of the Mexican boy Juan Darringo. He wasn't riding his burro. He had a fine Indian mustang and he rode as proud and straight as any man. After the episode in the Bosque Redondo, Flint had sought him out and put him on the payroll. Now, with the good food, he was filling out and muscling up and learning to handle the steers. A good investment, Flint thought.

Jason was riding along too, with his arm in a sling. And Marie was part of the outfit as well. She did a deal of cooking, which the boys appreciated. She had insisted on riding along when she saw nothing would hold Jason back.

Towards sundown Flint and Jason were riding alone. 'So they strung Remarque up,' Jason said as a matter of conversation. He and his father were still a little uneasy around one another.

'So I hear,' Flint said. That's one less killer in the land.'

Jason was looking off to the west where the sun rode

159

low over the hills. 'He deserved it, sure,' he said. 'He shouldn't have killed his sister that way.'

This was delicate territory. 'By his code Rosa Ramondo was a traitor. When she pulled that derringer he probably didn't stop to think. In his book she was working against him and that was enough.'

They rode on in silence for a while.

'She cut you loose in the cabin,' Flint said. 'You were all set to make your escape.'

Jason nodded abruptly. 'Sure,' he agreed. 'We aimed to ride off together, start a new life.'

Flint glanced at him sideways. 'That what she said?'

Jason avoided his eyes. 'She cut me loose. She didn't hold with all that killing. Wanted a new life for herself. When Fielder shot Cassidy she was sick to her stomach.'

Flint paused. 'She used Cassidy and that was wrong.'

Jason spoke up bravely. 'Sure she used Cassidy and that was a crime. Cassidy was a good man despite being weak.'

'And she would have used you,' Flint said.

Jason nodded grimly. 'Maybe, maybe not. Thing is she gave her life for me, and that's no small thing.'

Flint rode on in silence for a while. Coyotes started howling on the mesa. Ahead the boys were stopping. He could see the light of lanterns gleaming round the chuck wagon and knew that Marie was at work preparing supper. He knew it would be good.

'That's no small thing,' he agreed.

He reached out with his hand and grasped his son's good shoulder.